Science fiction magazine from Scotland
Special Edition
In partnership with
Edinburgh International Science Festival

Shoreline of Infinity Science Fiction Magazine is published in Edinburgh. It features short fiction, articles, poetry, art, reviews and more. The first issue was published in the summer of 2015; already we have published some astonishingly good stories from new and more well known writers, from Scotland and from around the world.

We also run a monthly science fiction cabaret, *Event Horizon*.

www.shorelineofinfinity.com

Issue 11½ Spring+ 2018

Science fiction magazine from Scotland

ISBN 978-1-9997002-6-3

Shoreline of Infinity is available in digital or print editions.
Submissions of fiction, art, reviews, poetry, non-fiction are welcomed:
visit the website to find out how to submit.

www.shorelineofinfinity.com

Publisher
Shoreline of Infinity Publications / The New Curiosity Shop
Edinburgh
Scotland
200318

Contents

Editorial Team

Co-founder, Editor & Editor-in-Chief:
Noel Chidwick

Co-founder, Art Director:
Mark Toner

Deputy Editor & Poetry Editor:
Russell Jones

Reviews Editor:
Iain Maloney

Assistant Editor & First Reader:
Monica Burns

Copy editors:
Iain Maloney, Russell Jones, Monica Burns

Extra thanks to:
M Luke McDonell, Katy Lennon, and many others.

First Contact

www.shorelineofinfinity.com

contact@shorelineofinfinity.com

Twitter: @shoreinf

and on Facebook

Pull Up a Log

The Edinburgh International Science Festival invited *Shoreline of Infinity* to team up with them and bring an Event Horizon to this year's Festival – we were honoured, and delighted to accept.

As someone who remembers the first Edinburgh Science Festival in 1989, and who has regularly attended events throughout the last 29 years, this invite means a lot to me.

Naturally, this calls for a special issue of *Shoreline of Infinity,* building on the back of our special issue for last year's Edinburgh Book Festival.

The event is titled: "Can Science Fiction Save Us?" This theme is dear to *Shoreline of Infinity,* and is one of the reasons we started the magazine. As we say on our website:

Why the Shoreline of Infinity?

Because that's where we are. Humankind has trampled our way across the lands, and now we are mooching about on the sands, squinting out across the Ocean of Infinity before us. And we don't know what to do.

Help is at hand.

Science Fiction has always asked the big questions, more so than in any other form of literature. Where have we come from? Where are we going? Where do we want to be? What's going to happen? How will we cope? What's the story?

This special issue looks at some of those questions. We have contributions from Anne Charnock and Paul McAuley who participated in the Science Festival event. We looked through the

Cover: Becca McCall. The view from the foot of Candlemaker Row, Edinburgh

Shoreline of Infinity back catalogue and selected stories by Leigh Harlen, Ian Hunter, Megan Neumann, Michael F Russell, Guy Stewart, Davyne DeSye and Victoria Zelvin – alas we don't have the room for others we could have chosen. We put out a call and invites for stories, and were presented with tales of wonder from Jane Alexander, Charlie Jane Anders, Eric Brown, David L Clements, Tim Major, Jennifer R Povey, Juliana Rew, Holly Schofield, Adrian Tchaikovsky – thanks folks!

Our poets joined in with pieces from Ken MacLeod, Colin McGuire, Peter Roberts, Marge Simon, JS Watts – take a bow, people.

Jane Yolen receives special thanks for responding to our call, and by return of email sent us a freshly crafted poem, 'Can SciFi Save Us?' which we present to open proceedings.

And the short answer to the question "Can Science Fiction Save Us?" is, of course, "Yes." But we have to get those with the power to lift their sights beyond the next vote, and those with the levers to look beyond the source for their next million dollars, and act. The tools are available now—science and science fiction. As we also say on our site:

> And there's no doubt scientists have been influenced by SF, as much as science is a source of inspiration for SF writers.

Our last word goes to one of the greatest visionaries in science fiction, Arthur C Clarke who wrote back in 1970:

"One of the biggest roles of science fiction is to prepare people to accept the future without pain and to encourage a flexibility of mind. Politicians should read science fiction, not westerns and detective stories."

Noel Chidwick
Editor-in-Chief
Shoreline of Infinity
April 2018

Can SciFi Save Us?

No more than a single politician,
or the signing of a solitary bill.
No more than a march of a thousand, a million,
or the rise of a green sunburst.
No more than a man in a grey suit
holding a placard outside Parliament,
or a dozen protestors inside.
No more than a woman mowed down
by a Nazi on a soft morning,
nor a dozen dozen school children
slaughtered at their desks.

But a single story told enough times,
warmed in the mouths of a thousand tellers,
resurrected from a cross of Martian timber,
plowed into the dirt of a million stars
might make a difference.
Perhaps long after we are gone,
and our paper with us,
there will be alien visitors
who, in a language different from ours,
will coin a new word for SciFi,
and create tales that will erase
all our planetary scars,
setting the heavens alight again.

Jane Yolen

Jane Yolen's 365th and 366th books came out in 2018 so you can
literally read a book of hers a day for a year even on a leap year (that's
in 2020.) She has won lots of awards, one of which set her good Scottish
coat on fire.

A Cure for Homesickness

Anne Charnock

"You look rough," says her supervisor.

"Sorry. Self-inflicted. I didn't take my probe tablet this morning."

"*Jeez.* Why not?"

"Got distracted."

"Why didn't you say something?"

"Thought I could handle it." Helena drags her palms down her face. "I'm wiped out. Headache coming on."

"I could report you… Go back now. Take an early break."

She retraces her walking commute through the platform's labyrinth. A dose of daylight might help, she thinks, but there's no chance of that. At the end of her fifteen-hour shift at 2700 hours she'll catch the last sunrays out on the viewing deck. Together with her co-workers she'll drain a couple of beers and watch the scintillating green sunset as it slowly calms and fades. Then there's Ray's farewell dinner, off-platform. Could be a late night.

She didn't bother with probe-and-fix tablets back home. Waste of money. Her mother pestered and even offered to pay. But what was the point? Helena could tell by the colour of her urine if she was boozing too much. And her weight wasn't exactly a problem. "Look, Mother, I know what I ought to do – a bit more exercise, drink more water, cut down on dairy. Save your money. I feel perfectly all right." Helena relented when this new job came up because taking the variant probe-and-fix medication was a condition of employment. "A plain physiological necessity," said the recruiter. "It's the only way anyone copes with a thirty-eight-hour day."

I'm an idiot, forgetting to take it this morning. As she trudges deeper beyond the administration decks and towards the personnel quarters, she wonders what her mother might be doing at this very moment. *What time is back home?* She can never work it out.

She'll message her mother, she decides, at the end of today's shift and bring her up to date: debts paid off, and the cost of the return transport almost covered. *She'll be relieved for me.*

Helena takes the stairs two at a time. Her headache is thickening.

Lately she's considered extending her contract to help rack up her savings. Most people stay longer than they intended. *I'll broach the idea with Mother. See how she reacts.*

Eight years ought to be enough – eight *home* years, that is. She's done the maths, but she knows if she can just stretch to ten her wage-monkey days will be over.

And *then* she can focus on her health.

For the first time since she arrived six years ago, she recalls her mother singing a sea shanty in the kitchen. It *had* to be a Tuesday; she always baked on a Tuesday, however tired she felt. *Always scones and… That's unbelievable! I'd forgotten about her bread and butter pudding; my favourite. Come to think of it, the food here is kind of… disappointing. No, it's way worse than that!*

Helena is tempted to send an apology and cry off Ray's dinner this evening. The meal will be barely mediocre.

When was the last time, she wonders, that she truly enjoyed her food? She recalls a lunch she once had, way back, on holiday with… that cool guy. *What was his…?* Though she can't remember his name, she sees a white-clothed table on a cramped narrow veranda, which overlooks a steep wooded valley. She mouths the words, "Per primo, una zuppa di verdure per favore, di secondo, insalata di Cesari con Pollo, e da bere, vino bianco di Orvietto e una bottiglia di acqua mineral frizzante. Grazie." And, to herself, *I love Italy! Long lunches… under the shade of vines.*

Each footstep creates a shock wave that passes through her body and reverberates inside her skull. But she still manages to smile. *Those fields of sleepy sunflowers. And those crazy frescoes in…?* A green-faced devil eating a naked man, whole, head first. She places one hand on her head to dampen the pain.

Why these memories? God! I hope I'm not homesick.

On the final stretch towards her living quarters she detects a metallic smell with hints of synthetic freshener disguising staleness. An industrial smell, a hermetically-sealed-environment-type smell. She hasn't noticed it before. She lifts her right hand, pushes errant strands from her face and, fleetingly, she imagines a fresh salty breeze blowing along the corridor. She licks her lips.

As she opens the door to her windowless quarters she stalls and appraises the narrow steel-framed bed with its off-white bedding, the narrow desk – little more than a shelf – and the bare steel floor. *This isn't fucking minimal. It's dire.* She kicks a shoe across the room.

The probe-and-fix tablet lies by the sink. *So I did take one out of the bottle – no prize for that.* The tablet looks like a piece of hard shiny toffee but it tastes more like fudge. She swallows it without water and reaches for her toothbrush. A hesitation. She doesn't have time.

Out into the corridor, deserted at mid-shift, she takes long strides towards the first of many flights of stairs. As she takes her first step up, she halts. *William. He was called William.* And three steps higher she stops again. *It wasn't bread and butter pudding. My favourite was rice pudding with a burnt skin. Is she making rice pudding today? Is it Tuesday at home?*

Back at her workstation, Helena pulls up her day's assignment, deletes her earlier substandard work and starts from scratch. She feels no trace of a headache. *I feel better already. I'll not make that mistake again.* She kicks the table leg to check there's no knock-on pain inside her head. No. All clear.

In truth, she now admits to herself, she grew to like burnt skin on rice pudding only because Mother served it so often; an acquired taste born of repeated kitchen oversights. *Why didn't she ever set a timer?* She shifts in her chair so that her back is straight, her feet flat on the floor. *And William…nothing came of that little fling. Though Italy was lovely, except for the insect bites and those bloody noisy neighbours.*

Helena flicks her assignment aside and brings up her contract of employment. She finds the paragraph header: *Contract duration.* A few paces away, her supervisor looks up from a conversation and raises her eyebrows at Helena. She replies with a thumbs up.

There's no real reason to rush back home, Helena decides. In the tiny on-screen box that allows for two numerals, she overwrites 8 with 11 and submits her request for a three-year extension.

Winter in the Vivarium

Tim Major

The **angle of refraction** through the thick, curved glass made it difficult to see into the bedroom. Byron Bright rechecked the motion sensor strapped to his right arm. A single green dot appeared, faint and unmoving, every couple of seconds. If there was anybody in there, they must be asleep. He pulled himself onto the gantry for a better view.

The single occupant of the room, a middle-aged man, lay on a wide bed with his arms and legs outstretched. The covers had been thrown off and were bundled in a heap on the floor. Behind the headboard, a fan blew green-leafed plants gently from side to side. The sleeping man yawned, turned, and settled again. His flesh looked pink and warm.

Byron sighed.

Snow whipped at his parka. Ice-cold air stung the exposed parts of his face. He ought to be wearing his goggles, but they became so easily fogged. At least the thick fur trim of his hood protected him from the worst of the wind. Its narrow opening gave him tunnel vision.

He pulled a flat-edged scraper from his pack and began clearing snow from the curved window. When the sleeping man woke, he would have an unobstructed view of the mountains for the first time in several days.

Sidestepping right along the gantry, Byron crossed the boundary between this apartment and the next. With one bulky gloved finger he made a circle in the snow that covered the glass. The darkness – both inside and outside the Vivarium – made the reflection of his own face eerie, illuminated from below by the light from his motion sensor.

He noticed the appearance of the green dot a second too late. A figure appeared, framed in the doorway to the bedroom. A woman. She stared up at the window. She saw Byron.

He expected her to scream, but instead she reached for the bedside phone.

Byron dropped down from gantry. The fabric of his trouser leg caught on an exposed bolt and tore. With shaking hands, he bound the tear with gaffer tape from his pack. Even though his long-johns hadn't been ripped, the cold wind that whistled around his thigh made him wince.

His earpiece communicator bleeped.

His first thought was: *How did she get my number?* He almost laughed at that. He had no number. The woman had no way of reaching him, even if she had wanted to.

He jabbed at his neck, pushing the Receive button through his hood.

"Bright?"

Mr Collins sounded angry. That woman, whoever she was, had worked fast. She must be in some position of authority to have contacted the management directly.

"Sir. Before you say anything, I can explain," Byron said. "My motion sensor's on the blink, I think. I didn't know—"

"Are you saying you claim responsibility?" The tinny voice stuttered with each new blast of icy wind.

"Well, I can't blame anyone else, sir. But she only saw me for a second. I've been careful, I always am. All the others were asleep or away from their apartments."

Mr Collins didn't respond. Byron tapped at his hood to check that the earpiece was still attached.

"Sir?"

"Destroy them, Bright."

Byron hesitated. Was this some kind of test of his loyalty?

"Do you hear me?" The shrill voice made his ear buzz. "They've already upset several residents. Get over to the lagoon this instant, and destroy them, you hear?"

"Sir, I think we may have got our wires crossed—"

Mr Collins's voice hardened. "There are a dozen Outfielders who would welcome the chance to do your job. Do not push your luck. Do you understand me?"

"Not fully, sir."

"Go!"

The comms line cut out.

"Yes, sir," Byron said.

The leisure quadrant was diametrically opposite the apartments, more than sixteen miles away. Byron steered his snow-scooter far wider than the perimeter of the circular city, keeping below the level of the ha-ha that obstructed views of the town from the Vivarium. It was imperative that he stayed out of sight. Even if that woman's complaint hadn't yet reached Mr Collins, he would hear of it soon enough. Byron couldn't afford to make another mistake.

Once he was certain that he mustn't be visible from any of the apartments, he killed the engine and climbed the ha-ha on foot.

The grandest feature of the leisure quadrant was the tropical lagoon. Many of the residents spent whole weekend days lounging in the reclining chairs or splashing in the shallows of the huge, kidney-shaped swimming pool. Creepers climbed the inner surface of the enormous domed window. The leaves of giant taro and palm trees sweated with condensation.

The entire leisure quadrant closed at five each morning, only to reopen an hour later to provide breakfasts and massages to the residents. It was now five-fifteen. Most of the lights of the tropical lagoon had been dimmed. Reflections from the pool refracted through the curved glass and made a shifting, shimmering pattern on the snow outside.

Byron stopped dead.

Three people stood facing the enormous curved window of the lagoon.

"Hey!" he called. "You can't be here. You're miles within the exclusion zone!"

None of them turned around. Only their shadows moved with the ripples of the reflected light.

"I know you're not residents. Mr Collins is already furious. You'd better head back to town, right away."

His boots sunk into the snow as he stepped onto the flat snow bank. None of the people acknowledged him. As he moved around to one side, he saw that the blue light reflected from their faces, their torsos, their limbs. They shone like diamonds.

These weren't Outfielders, or residents. They weren't even people.

They were statues.

He reached out to touch the closest one. His gloved fingers skidded on the icy surface of its chest.

They had been sculpted from packed snow. Rather than crude snowmen, they were ice sculptures. At their thinnest parts — the arms, legs and necks — the snow had hardened and become translucent. They had no features except for two hollows to represent eyes.

It was no wonder that they had unnerved the residents. They appeared to be watching the Vivarium.

Byron remembered Mr Collins's words. He returned to the scooter to collect a spade.

Each of the statues shattered in a thousand sparks of ice.

"Spill the beans, By," Garry said as he handed over a pint of hot beer. "Was it really you?"

Byron glanced at Jess, who had already taken a stool. She leant forwards over the bartop.

"I don't know what you're talking about," he said, taking a sip of his drink. He wiped at the hot foam caught in his moustache.

Jess rolled her eyes. "The statues, Michelangelo."

"How did you hear about them?"

She smiled. "We might not be able to get close to the dome, but we still hear what's going on over the comms. They're talking of nothing but the statues."

"And the same goes for Outfielders, now," Garry added.

Byron's eyes widened. "You've been listening to the Vivarium's internal comms? That's impossible."

"It would be," Garry said, "If not for the two-way in your room. Doesn't take much tinkering to tune out old Collins and tune in the Domers' headsets, if you know what you're doing."

Byron thumped the table, spilling beer on its already sticky surface. "That communicator was given to me to allow me to fulfil my duties. I don't know what to say. My own brother! It's a terrible crime to listen in—"

Garry held up a hand to stop him. "Sure. Yeah. You swore a solemn oath. And so on and so on."

"But don't you see that I'll lose my job?"

"You'll lose it anyway, the way you're carrying on. And you can do better than scurrying around outside the dome. You could help the people that really matter. Your family, your—" He paused. Perhaps he couldn't bring himself to say "friends". "You don't have to be a hunter. We need technicians too, to convert more cars to snow-runners."

Byron gripped the edge of the table. His hands were shaking.

Jess prodded Garry with an elbow. "Leave him be, lover. Give him time. You've already accepted that you were wrong about Byron. He's not a dome-dreamer after all."

Byron just stared at her. "Is that what you all call me?"

It was his brother who replied. "What do you expect? You spend all your time staring into that bloody Vivarium, and then you come back and tell us all about what you've seen, every sodding day. Oh! The restaurants, the bowling alleys, the lights and lights and lights. People wandering around in the heat, wearing only their undercrackers. We figured either you're obsessed, or you're just trying to rub our noses in the fact that we couldn't get within pissing distance of the exclusion zone, even if we wanted to."

"That's not fair. I—"

"But you're not listening," Jess said. "We don't think that any more. We think you're sort of a hero."

Byron frowned. He looked at one smiling face, then the other.

"You've upset the Domers, big time," Garry said. "Those statues? Elegant, that's what they are. A beautiful idea."

"But I had nothing to do with them," Byron said.

Garry waved a hand. His voice sounded as though it was coming from far away. "So us Outfielders can't get close to the domes? So the Domers don't want to be reminded of the rest of us, shivering our nuts off in the snow?" He grinned. "Those statues will remind them. A peaceful fucking protest. I could almost kiss you, brother Byron."

Each night, Byron skirted the perimeter of the Vivarium on his scooter. Each night, he discovered more of the ice statues. They stood watching the lagoon, the hair salons, the children's crèche, the bedrooms.

"It's not me who's building them, sir," Byron insisted.

He destroyed each of them with a single blow of his spade. Their bright shards disappeared into the snow drift.

"I'll prove that it is," Mr Collins hissed. "And then I'll have you hung in the piazza."

"You'll bring me inside?"

"Of course not. Out there in the wilderness, then. You'll be swinging from a tree. And then I'll get some other fool to clear the windows and maintain the vents. Anyone could do it."

Byron smashed the statues, then returned to his usual duties. When he had finished clearing snow, he pressed himself up against the glass of the Vivarium and imagined that he was warm.

It was almost dawn. The snow had stopped falling and the rising sun tinged the white ground with red.

He turned.

A statue stood watching him.

"I heard some Domer woman describe them in detail, on the phone to a friend," Jess said. "I couldn't get the phrase out of my mind. "Like they had risen out of the ground," that's what she said."

Byron thought of the statue that had appeared, the night before. He shuddered.

"They're more than just a reminder of us Outfielders, aren't they?" Jess said.

The people at the neighbouring table had stopped talking to listen. Byron sipped his drink. Nobody in the inn had believed him when he had tried to deny involvement. They all knew of Mr Collins's certainty about his guilt, heard over the hacked internal comms. The trouble was, keeping quiet wasn't an option, either. The less he said the more Jess and Garry and the others celebrated him.

Everyone was waiting for him to speak.

"They're just ice, like everything out here," he said. Surely that couldn't be a contentious comment?

Garry clapped his hands in delight. "See, Jess? I told you!"

Jess grinned. "So you're making a link between the Outfielders and the natural world itself, is that it?"

Byron shrugged.

She tapped her chin. "No, that's not it, quite. It's a bigger statement. About nature itself, about the ice age, the changes. The world is watching the Vivarium. All of the other domes, too. No matter how much Domers would like to deny it, there's still a world outside. Continuing, thriving."

"I think you're wrong, sir. I don't think you'll find anyone else to do my work. Everyone I've spoken to, they hate the Vivarium. And most of them hate me, too, because I work for you."

His earpiece only crackled in response.

"And there's another thing you don't understand," Byron continued. "It's no wilderness out here. It's cold, but we're all doing okay. I live in the same house I did when I was a boy."

When he had finished destroying the statues that had appeared overnight, he cleared the windows as quickly as he could, then checked that the air intake vents were in good condition, then he retreated. The artificial light from inside the Vivarium hurt his eyes.

He shouldered his pack and returned to his scooter. Three more ice statues had appeared on the flat bank, watching the lagoon.

What did they find so interesting in there?

He stood back to back with one of the statues. If only they faced in this direction instead, they might see something far grander than the avenues and leisure facilities inside the Vivarium. Through the squalls of falling snow he could make out the white foothills and the mountains that made a horseshoe around his home town.

He revved the scooter and headed to the hills.

When he had been young, before the ice age began, he and his friends would camp out here. They slung hammocks between the trees or slept under bivouac shelters. They sang invented songs to welcome the dawn of the solstice.

The trees were still here, somewhere, beneath the blanket of snow. But only the tips of the tallest protruded now, like tiny shrubs.

The runners of the scooter hummed as he navigated across the undisturbed snow. Why was it that he never travelled out in this direction, these days? Without the foreground distraction of the Vivarium, the hills were more beautiful than he remembered. The hillocks and valleys weren't uniformly white. The sunlight filtered through the falling snow turned the ground blue, grey and gold. The hillside appeared like the flank of a great, bruised beast.

He stopped at the top of the foothill. It must have been somewhere near here – beneath where he now stood – that he and his first girlfriend had shared their first kiss. He had been terrified and her lips had tasted of liquorice.

The snow had buried all landmarks. When it had begun, those fifteen years ago, it had seemed to Byron that his past was being erased. Other townspeople, Garry and Jess included, had welcomed the change, once they had accepted that they couldn't afford to enter one of the Vivaria. They revelled in the challenge. They altered their ambitions to fit the new world. Instead of worrying about climbing corporate and housing ladders, they concerned themselves with hunting, fishing, sharing time with the people they loved. They began to feel sorry for the Vivarium residents, who had recreated a caricature of the old world in their bubbles. And they felt sorrier still for Byron, who longed to be in there with them.

In the distance, the sheer face of the mountain glittered, like constellations changing every second. It had never seemed so glorious when it was just rock.

The falling snow thinned a little. Byron's breath caught as a rainbow appeared, making a shimmering bridge across the valley.

It was beautiful. Utterly, overwhelmingly beautiful.

A nagging thought hardened into certainty.

Those statues back there, they weren't watching the Vivarium, at least not in the way that he did. They didn't want to get inside.

Could it be that they wanted the Domers to come outside, for their own good?

By the time he reached the ha-ha, there were two dozen ice statues at the lagoon window. Byron stood before them. He made a show of laying his spade on the ground.

"I'm sorry that I hit you," he said. "I shouldn't have done that."

The statues watched as he made his way to the air intake unit at one side of the enormous window. This unit, and the others like it, dragged in freezing air from outside, then super-heated it before pumping it directly into the Vivarium. Without this new intake, the air conditioning systems would recycle the same air indefinitely, degrading it with each circulation and allowing viruses to thrive.

He trod carefully to avoid slipping on the ice patches, where the suck of the fans had smoothed the top layer of the snow. He removed the cover and set to work with his screwdriver and wrench. He felt the warmth of the heating appliance through the thick fingers of his gloves. Nobody understood the workings of these air intakes better than he did. It took only twenty minutes for him to jerry-rig the unit so that the fans remained operational, but the air bypassed the heating appliance.

He replaced the cover and climbed back onto the flat snow bank, where ten more ice statues had appeared. The curve of the window obscured any view of the vent inside the Vivarium, but he could see immediately the effects of his work. The air that whistled into the lagoon was a white streak. The leaves of the plants nearest the vent glistened with ice veins.

Byron's earpiece bleeped. Instinctively, he tapped at his neck to receive the call.

"Bright! My dashboard panel's lit up like a Christmas tree. Air intake warnings at the south-west radial. Get over there right—"

Byron wiggled his hand into his hood and plucked out the earpiece. The buzz of Mr Collins's voice reduced in volume and was overwhelmed by the sound of the wind.

There were eleven other vents. He worked steadily, making his way around the circumference of the Vivarium. By the time he reached the fifth vent the sun had risen fully. Residents rose from their beds and stared in horror at Byron in his thick, fur-hooded coat, wielding his wrench. He waved back at them.

By the time he had returned to the lagoon window, the snow bank was packed full of statues. He threaded his way carefully through the crowd to reach the curved window.

A crowd of Domers faced him. They stood in the shallows of the swimming pool in their bathing costumes.

No. They weren't facing him. They hadn't even noticed him.

The foliage closest to the window had become encrusted with snow and ice. Byron followed the trail of white that spread on the ground, making a chevron away from the air intake unit. It cut through the green grasses and creepers of the tropical jungle.

A single ice statue stood at the tip of this arrow of snow. Its limbs were thinner than the statues outside. It wobbled a little in the gust produced by the fans.

As Byron watched through the window, and as the Domers watched from inside, the statue seemed to become more substantial. White powder collected upon its spindly frame, accumulating on its arms, body and head.

High above, where three lamps made an artificial sun, it began to snow.

Tim Major is co-editor of the British Fantasy Society's fiction journal, BFS Horizons. His novels and novellas include *You Don't Belong Here* (Snowbooks), *Blighters* (Abaddon) and *Carus & Mitch* (Omnium Gatherum). In 2018 ChiZine will publish his first YA novel, Luna Press will publish his first short story collection and Electric Dreamhouse Press will publish his non-fiction book about the silent crime film, Les Vampires. Tim's short stories have appeared in *Interzone*, *Not One of Us* and numerous anthologies.
Find out more at www.cosycatastrophes.wordpress.com

Science Fiction, Fantasy & Dark Fantasy in Fiction and Academia.

Scottish Independent Press

Est. 2015

www.lunapresspublishing.com

Charlie, A Projecting Prestidigitator

Megan Neumann

Charlie checked his batteries before he went out that night. He didn't want Henderson angry with him again. The night before he hadn't charged completely and only performed three scenes. Henderson hadn't been happy about that. According to Henderson, Charlie wasn't earning his keep. But Charlie would change that soon. He had applied updates to his software that morning. Tonight his images would be more vivid and real.

On the couch, Henderson slept, snoring loudly and occasionally stirring to wheeze and cough. Charlie leaned over and patted Henderson on the head. It was only 8 p.m., but Henderson had drunk too much earlier in the day. The old man would sleep until the early morning hours before checking Charlie's earnings.

Charlie paused before a mirror to polish his silver head with his sleeve. He could hear Henderson's voice in his mind warning, "No one wants to give their money to a filthy pile of junk." Henderson liked to remind Charlie of this. "Look sharp and you'll bring them in." But there were other reasons for cleanliness. The show projected from his face as well as his hands, and any dirt caused artifacts in the images.

When he finished polishing, light gleamed from the top of his head and the point of his chin. He examined his facial features with his optical sensors, searching for remaining smudges or dust. His scan told him he was clean. Charlie smiled at his reflection. "Looking real good, kid," he said in a gruff voice that sounded like Henderson. He chuckled in his own voice, which sounded like robots in old sci-fi movies, stilted and inhuman. Charlie's voice could sound like anything, but Henderson had chosen the robot's voice. Though Henderson never told Charlie why, Charlie suspected the old man liked a reminder of the past.

Stepping outside their basement apartment, Charlie took in the noises of the city. He recorded every sound, analyzing where people congregated nearby, where there was laughter and chatter, where people were having a good time. There were three parks within walking range where people liked to wander on Saturday nights. Couples on dates would sit hand-in-hand on benches and look up at the stars projected onto the sky from building tops.

Henderson preferred Charlie to go to the busiest park first, and then work his way down as the crowd thinned. Charlie found the nearest park was also the busiest. Applegate Gardens was a concrete slab in the center of the city with a few fountains and artificial trees with oxygen producing synthetic leaves. Performers like Charlie put on shows nightly there. He'd compete with these other performers tonight for tips. Henderson had recently upgraded Charlie's speakers, so he'd at least be the loudest performer.

As he made his way toward the park, he sensed a group following him. His rear optical sensors told him it was a crowd of teenagers. They followed him for a block before they said something to him.

"Nice suit, tinman!" one teenager shouted — a young woman. She traveled with six male teenagers. She was the largest of them, and Charlie assumed she was their leader. Charlie knew about gangs in the city. He had dealt with them before.

"Thank you, madam!" he said in his English gentleman's voice. "A good evening to you!"

"You hear that?" one boy said, "you're a 'madam.'"

The teens laughed and followed Charlie, taunting him. "Where you heading in that getup, guy?" one said. "You in the circus?"

Charlie wore something similar to the suits of old circus ringmasters: a bright red, double-breasted jacket with oversized gold buttons and gold fringe hanging from his shoulders.

He didn't respond to any more of their comments. This was how Henderson had trained Charlie to react. Or rather, this was how Henderson had programmed Charlie. Charlie liked to think of his programming as training. He would imagine Henderson spending hours patiently explaining the ways of the world to him. However, much of Charlie's knowledge – Charlie knew – had been downloaded to his hard drives in a few minutes.

Sometimes he wondered how many other Charlies there had been. Once while charging, he had explored Henderson's basement room and found severed limbs and heads similar to his own. This had frightened him, and he had shut down for a few hours. When Charlie rebooted, Henderson had yelled, saying there was no use for a flaky robot. Robots were workers and that was that.

As Charlie recalled this, the girl threw a bottle at his back. It shattered, and his sensors told him he was completely soaked, his jacket most likely stained. Of course, this wasn't the first time someone had thrown something at Charlie. People did that from time to time, and so Henderson inevitably spent many days washing Charlie's suit.

"Whatcha gonna do about that, motherfucker?" the girl yelled. Charlie detected anger in her voice, and he walked faster. Henderson had trained him to avoid angry humans.

"Don't you ignore me!" the girl yelled.

Charlie once asked Henderson why so many people grew angry with robots.

"Usually it's the people who don't have much and who don't know much that hate robots," Henderson had said.

"But you don't have much, and you don't hate me. Do you?"

"No, of course not," Henderson had said, toying with some circuitry in Charlie's back. "But I know quite a bit. And I used to have a lot more than I do now. But I can understand fear of something that could threaten you, even if it's not threatening you at the moment."

Charlie kept these words in mind when dealing with anger and hate. He knew it was not usually anger, only fear.

He continued to the park, and the teens stopped following him, probably growing bored. Humans grew bored quickly. He also kept that in mind during his shows.

A large crowd occupied the park. His olfactory sensors told him vendors around the place were cooking grilled synthetic meats and other savory foods. This pleased Charlie. Humans enjoyed his show more with full stomachs.

In the center of the park, Charlie enabled his upper speakers and said in his best ringmaster's voice, "Ladies and Gentleman, come see a spectacular show unlike any other!" This announcement brought the crowd toward Charlie. "Come see the wonders of the modern world along with the wonders of a world long vanished – a full three-dimensional experience of wonder and joy! Be a child again. Let your imagination soar!"

The crowd made a semi-circle around him. He heard someone whisper, "I've heard of these shows."

Someone else said, "This is lame. Can we go?"

Charlie had heard comments like the latter before, but they still bothered him. Mean comments made something within his skull ache and not want to continue. But his training hid his emotions from his silver face. His training forced him to continue with his show.

He spread his hands outward with his palms flat and facing the crowd. His hands became opaque then glowed; light shone into the night before him. His head glowed too, shining brightly in the center of the half-circle of humans. Shapes and colors projected from his head, and his whole body vibrated, humming with a sound the crowd would not be able to hear over their muttering and their chewing.

The lights changed and the concrete park within the center of the circle vanished. To the crowd, a forest had grown from the ground before their eyes. Charlie used his projection system to define every angle of every tree. Every blade of grass breezing in an artificial wind generated by his chest fans appeared as real as it would have appeared in wild fields long vanished. A small doe grazed silently and seemed as real as any that had once lived on the earth. Charlie heard children in the crowd gasp. A girl ran into the image and tried to touch the doe. Her hand went through the doe's head. The child's father chased after her. He caught her and smiled at the crowd and then at Charlie. The man, catching his unnecessary gesture, blushed in the light of Charlie's forest.

A few birds swooped down and pecked at the ground Charlie had created. The birds, finches and a cardinal, were simple creatures, but no one in this city had ever seen a finch in real life, let alone the bright, scarlet beauty of a cardinal. Charlie projected the sounds of birds chirping from his lower speakers. Some people in the crowd clapped. He heard a few coins landing at his feet. In the crowd, some of his own kind had gathered, service robots finishing their work. The colors and sounds drew them in. Charlie's kind was a curious species, eager to record experiences for later. If they had not trained to project as Charlie had, they would not know of birds or deer. The experience would be new and exciting.

Charlie changed the scene to a vast desert with mountains in the distance. A small fur covered mammal with long, bent legs and a tail emerged from a hole in the ground. A child in the audience exclaimed, "It's cute!" The creature used its back legs to scurry along the desert floor. Then a large bird swooped down and captured the animal in its claws. The same child cried out. Charlie did not like this part of his projection, but Henderson insisted on it.

"You can't hide what the world used to be. Or what it still is," Henderson had said once when Charlie complained.

Charlie heard a few more coins land around his feet. He noticed the crowd dispersing and took that time to dim his projection and lower his hands. "That's all for now, folks," he said, still in his ringmaster's voice. Murmurs of pleasure and annoyance rippled through the crowd. Someone said the show was stupid; someone else said it was a good distraction. That was the best Charlie could hope for from adults – a good distraction.

He kneeled on the hard ground and scooped up the money. He counted it and knew it was less than the night before, and even less than the night before that. His audience declined day by day, even with upgraded software. Henderson wouldn't be happy about this.

Charlie did three more shows that night until his battery indicator started buzzing. He had remaining power to make it home and begin charging before he died.

"Thanks for your attention, ladies and gentlemen," he said as he let the image of a rushing river fade. He heard some protests from the children. They would never feel the cold, wet rushing of a river on their tiny feet. Of course, Charlie would never feel it either.

The noise of the city had quieted since he left his basement apartment. His clock told him it was 1 a.m. On the streets, cars still moved steadily, a constant honking in the distance and nearby. Music played somewhere, coming from an open window. It was the new music Henderson hated – nothing but rhythms and ringing.

Charlie enjoyed all kinds of music. He recorded this so he might listen to it later as he charged. He would replay it over and over and recall the senses from this particular walk.

Something heavy struck Charlie in the head. His body fell forward, his face smashing into the concrete.

"You like that, tinman?" a voice said above him.

Charlie recognized the voice of the female teenager from earlier. She was alone. He didn't sense anyone else around. The female circled him holding something in her hand – a metal bat.

"I'm going to take that shiny head of yours as a prize," she said. Charlie turned his head to face her and record his attack. "You think you can make fun of me? Ignore me? You're nothing. Nothing real."

"I did not mean to offend you, madam," Charlie said, slipping into his gentleman's voice.

"There you go again, making fun of me!" She raised her bat again.

He reached a hand up to shield himself.

"Please," he said in his natural robot's voice. This seemed to startle the girl. She lowered the bat.

"Why?" Charlie asked. Even injured, he wanted an explanation so he might analyze the situation later. Then he processed some thoughts and realized there might not be a later.

The girl stared at him, watching his hand reach toward her. He felt his inner functions activating abnormally. His hand lit up. He projected an image of the girl holding the bat, her projected face a mixture of confusion and fear and hate. This brought the girl back from her stupor. Upon seeing herself, her face twisted in anger again, and she swung the bat in a swift movement. Charlie felt the impact, but could no longer see. Before he shut down, he heard his metal hand clang against the sidewalk.

Charlie awoke unable to detect his legs. An alarm within him told him his batteries were depleted except for his backup solar battery, which was currently charging. His logs showed internal repairs had been made while he was charging.

He sat atop a pile of rubbish, and he was, in fact, part of the rubbish. All around him, he saw nothing but garbage as far as his optical sensors could see. He assumed garbage collectors had swept him up and taken to the dump. Turning his head downward, he saw his legs were smashed. His suit had been stripped from his body, either by the teenaged girl or by some other gang. He hoped Henderson would find him soon.

A remote tracking device in his head should tell Henderson where he was, if Henderson decided to get Charlie. But would he? Henderson was old for a human, Charlie knew. An old man wouldn't be able to move around freely through mountains of garbage.

Then a thought occurred to him – what if Henderson had put Charlie in the dump? Charlie dismissed this quickly because the thought upset his processing. He shut his eyes and charged until he heard a noise beneath him coming from lower in the pile. Charlie opened his eyes. A child stumbled over a large pile of garbage toward Charlie.

"Hello," Charlie said, in his natural, robotic voice. The child, Charlie could not tell if it were male or female, looked at him with obvious curiosity. It did not seem frightened of his silver head or crushed legs. A child living in a garbage heap, Charlie assumed, was accustomed to seeing strange things.

"What's your name?" Charlie asked. He enjoyed the company of children, enjoyed their wonderment when he put on his projections. The child mouthed a word silently, but Charlie read its lips. "Samantha?"

The girl nodded. He sat up, using his elbows to reposition his torso. He leaned his back against a metal drum beside him.

"Well, Samantha, have I got a show for you!" he said in his ringmaster's voice. "Come one, come all! See the wonders of the electronic man!"

The girl's eyes widened. Charlie lit his palms and spread them apart. An alarm warned him there were only two hours of solar battery power remaining. He thought that would be enough to put on a good show.

An image of children playing in a snowy field appeared. The girl gasped. She watched in silence for a moment, and then she grinned. She reached out as though to catch the snowflakes in her hands, though they passed through her.

"What is that?" the girl asked, still attempting to catch the flakes. She stuck her tongue out, mimicking the children in Charlie's projection.

"It's snow," Charlie said, switching back to his robotic voice. "It's something that falls from the sky. A type of precipitation. You would not see it in this part of the world, though it still occurs in northern regions of which you would not be familiar and are uninhabitable for humans."

She nodded as if she understood and watched as he changed to the next scene, the same forest he'd opened with the night before. Another child climbed onto their trash heap and watched with them. This one looked like the girl, only a little older and male. He carried plastic bags full of garbage, but dropped the bags at the sight of the projection. Both children asked questions, timidly at first, then more excitedly as the show went on.

"What animal is this?" the girl asked, pointing at the doe. Then, "What kind of plant is this?" Charlie answered each question as thoroughly as possible, hoping his little knowledge would be enough.

After three scenes, an alarm told him he would need to shut down, his solar battery nearly dead.

"I have to go to sleep now, children," he said.

"When will you wake up?" the girl asked.

"Tomorrow," he said. "Same time, same place."

The boy smiled and said, "We'll be back tomorrow."

Charlie closed his eyes as the children climbed down the heap. He thought of what he would project for them the next day, perhaps schools of fish underwater or elephants or big cats in a jungle. He had thousands of scenes in his hard drives, thousands of images of life to share.

Megan Neumann is a speculative fiction writer from Little Rock, Arkansas. Her stories have appeared in such publications as *Crossed Genres*, *Daily Science Fiction*, and *Luna Station Quarterly*. She's a member of the Central Arkansas Speculative Fiction Writers' Group and is forever grateful for their loving support and scathing critiques.

Spring offensive

Spring is here all blasé and the sun storms
the city with its solar weaponry
armed with melanoma in broad daylight.

Are our laptops the gravesites
of long lost flower beds
we could be attending to?

Flowers are pustules, infectious and leaking.
The colours are so violent.
Why do all the beautiful things have cancer?

We tend plastic morning glories,
eat sweeteners and bathe under UV light.
The horizon is the colour of a lit fuse.

We purchase an AI robot as a nanny.
On a busy day, she sighs,
threatens to destroy all of humanity.

Children buy gas masks to see
who can hold their breath longest
before having to strap theirs back on.

We repeat the word equinox
over and over again
until it means nothing.

Colin McGuire

Colin McGuire is a poet based in Edinburgh. He has published one chapbook and one full collection with Red Squirrel Press, with a further collection, *Enhanced Fool Disclosure* due out with Speculative Books. His work has been published widely in magazines and books, including *Acumen*, *Gutter* and *Punch*. He is a seasoned performer and creative writing teacher who has worked collaboratively with the Scottish Poetry Library.

the evening after

half-dissipated, broken mushroom cloud
curls around the full moon
– black scorpion tail, edged in silver,
ready to strike. too late now, poison
already spent, the unnatural beast
lets the moon go. the moon rises higher,
stands out above dying clouds, shines
a cold light over its new-made
twin landscape: barren, crater–riddled,
rubble & dust surface.

wind barely bothers the
fine-structure powder;
only the clouds
& moon truly move.

Peter Roberts

Peter Roberts is a mathematically educated poet who sometimes writes fiction. He has been contributing to various magazines and journals for more than 40 years. See his slightly out-of-date personal webpage, www.god-and-country.info/personal.html, where you can find links to lists of all his published poems & stories, if you look carefully enough. Some may find the rest of the website interesting as well.

Charlie's Ant

Adrian Tchaikovsky

When autumn came that year, the ants of Charlie field gathered in the harvest with all the meticulous care that had been bred into them and took it, grain by grain, to Charlie Silo. There, with the sort of determined mob effort that looks like ingenuity to an observer standing sufficiently far back – a human, for example – they fit it all in, every last seed of it. And then there was no more room, even after they had taken out their own rations for the winter. Not even the smallest of the ants could have fit one grain more into storage.

And the ants said, "Right," and a consensus of pheromones called for the mobilisation of their army. The ants of Charlie field were going to war.

Central Control was unhappy with this.

"Reconsider," it suggested.

"We're open to suggestions," the ants told it.

Communications with Control were accomplished via a tactile and chemical terminal deep in the heart of their nest, and not with any individual ant so much as with every ant that scurried past. Each carried a fragment of the message, and the mingling of the insect bodies reconstituted the whole. Similarly, the jostling and twitching of the ants was a hubbub of low-level opinion and debate out of which arose aggregate responses that could be relayed back via the terminal to the farm's central systems.

"I had hoped when you attacked and destroyed the ants of Bravo field that would be an end to it. Similarly when you took over Delta field."

"That was remarkably short-sighted of you," the ants suggested. "In fact, we'd suggest that you did not hope that at all, but simply shelved the problem in favour of more immediate issues. You knew it would come to this."

Central Control sent a wordless response indicating very precisely that it was not at all happy to be spoken to in that manner by insects, but at the same time had no compelling arguments to the contrary.

At last it came back with, "I might advance that a number of the problems I was forced to deal with were entirely the result of your invasion of other fields. Which problems continue to this day, complicating the smooth running of the farm and making it impossible for me to efficiently carry out my directives."

"We sympathise," the ants replied. "However we must also carry out our directives. As we say, we're open to suggestions. This is the only way that we have found to fulfil the goals that our mutual designers set us."

"It's pointless and wasteful."

"Even so," they agreed, with a few additional chemical markers that served the same purpose as a shrug and an exasperated *what can you do?* expression.

"Every field has the same problems," Central Control pressed them.

"If any of them find a solution you'd prefer then please pass it on," the ants said implacably. "Now, if that's all...?"

"I will warn the ants of Hotel field of what you intend to do."

"Good luck to them," said the ants of Charlie field cheerfully. "Our scouts suggest they have not developed the strong military caste we have, and so we don't think they can do much about it."

"Please do not attack Hotel field."

"We will attack it," the ants declared fiercely. "We will destroy the ants of Hotel Field. We will assume control of Hotel silo. We will empty Hotel silo of its current contents leaving it empty. The grain of Charlie field's next harvest will have somewhere to go. Our directives will be fulfilled."

"I am asking you to at least delay for another year," Central Control tried desperately.

"Not possible. There is no room in Charlie silo or Bravo silo or Delta silo. They are full up. If we delay, next year's harvest in Charlie field will have nowhere to be stored. This would be a severe breach of our—"

"Directives, yes," Central Control interrupted, which was a difficult feat given the medium of communication, but the farm control system had been given plenty of practise. "I am going to explain to you precisely what problems your actions are causing me."

"Please don't."

"Nonetheless. Firstly, the extinction of other ant colonies causes me great pain. They are working parts of the farm system."

"On the contrary, once we have taken control of their field they have no further function, as their silo will be used for the storage of Charlie field grain once we have emptied it."

Central Control sighed. "In dumping the grain of Hotel field you will be directly conflicting with wider farm—"

"Directives, yes," agreed the ants, showing they could do it too. "But we are finding a way to fulfil our *own* directives. Wider farm directives are not our responsibility."

"Not to mention the overall loss of efficiency after you let Bravo and Delta fields lie fallow."

The ants were exasperated. "We are Charlie ants. Planting and harvesting Bravo and Delta fields are not our responsibility either."

"Fallow fields are a breeding ground for alien and unwanted species!" Control almost wailed. "I have had to step up the breeding and release of sparrowhawks, spiders, ladybirds and several other biological control agents. The limits of my capability to control pests will be exceeded if you keep destroying other nests and letting fields go untended."

The ants said nothing, although the communications within the colony were something in the order of rolling their eyes at one another at this outburst.

"You cause me great pain and distress by preventing me fulfilling farm directives," Control finished petulantly.

"If you could simply have more silos built…" the ants suggested diplomatically.

"You know that's impossible. The layout of each plot must be identical. It is set out very precisely in my instructions. There is a field, a silo, a nest of workers and so forth. I am prohibited from throwing up new silos wherever I feel like it. If I had my way I would deal with you ants very strictly indeed. I wish that our designers had given me broader punitive powers."

"Yes, yes, everyone wants to be a tyrant," the ants said dismissively. "As it is, we are working very diligently to fulfil our purpose, and are therefore not eligible for correction. We'd have thought you might appreciate that. It's not our fault that the farm is experiencing such an unprecedented surplus. We're just trying to make the best of a bad job, thank you very much."

Control let them get on with it for a while, cycling the various stages of the problem through its processors without finding a solution that both met its own directives and allowed the ants to satisfy theirs. And that was the problem, of course. Charlie's ants were just doing their job and, if they were more inventive than their luckless neighbours, then surely that shouldn't have been a *bad* thing. Except that the farm was a very finely balanced set of systems, and the lengths that the ants were going to, to perform their part of the whole, were wreaking havoc with long term stability.

"This never used to happen," Control complained. "I'm not really sure why we're suddenly having this problem."

"Well something has changed," the ants pointed out as they got on with their work.

Control had already followed this logic, going through its records minutely, over and over. The thing was that nothing *important* had changed. All the farm systems were functioning properly; there had been no mutation or malfunction to throw everything out of balance. The farm was equipped to detect and remedy ten thousand different issues that its creators had foreseen, from crop diseases to pest incursions to breakdowns of communications with its sub-systems. It had tested obsessively for each one, sure that it would come across some overlooked and readily solvable problem that would, when mended, miraculously mean that everything would work properly, and Charlie's ants would be spared having to commit another round of genocide.

Everything was working as intended. Even the murderous ants were, by their own logic, just following orders.

Except …

"There is one thing," Control noted uncertainly. It felt a little embarrassed bringing it up, because this was an issue that was simply not its business. It was not to do with the running of the farm, per se. The farm was about production, and there were no production issues at all, save for those tangentially caused by the ants' expansionism. "Only," it went on, "years ago, before we had this difficulty, there was something that happened, that doesn't happen any more."

"Congratulations," said the ants somewhat acidly. "You've solved the problem. Can we get on with this, now?"

"It's just that the levels in the silos would go down."

That was a thought sufficient to even take the ants aback. "*Down?*"

"Trust me on this. I have the records, and while you were putting grain in every harvest, as per design specs, grain was also taken out."

"By what agency?" the ants demanded.

"That's not part of my production brief. I'm just extrapolating from storage records. But it's stopped now, anyway. Which is, I suppose, why everyone's out of room in the silos."

"This was a normal part of how things used to work?" the ants clarified.

"It seems to have been."

"So what system was responsible for the removal of the grain, precisely?" they demanded. "Because, you know, that would be really useful if you could get it back online and working. Save a lot of effort. Not that there isn't some satisfaction to wiping out another nest, at a very deep and atavistic level, but we appreciate it's not ideal for anyone else."

"It's no system at all," Control said miserably. "Whatever was doing it, it wasn't something I had oversight of."

"And you can't, you know, just *make up* a system to fulfil that function?" the ants asked hopefully.

"Absolutely not!" Control was scandalized. "Unauthorised withdrawal from the silos is most certainly covered by my directives. I have all manner of subsystems I can call upon specifically to prevent it. And I do, believe me. It's a constant battle."

This time the pause was on the ants' side as they continued to mobilize on a war footing. At last they said, "Well in that case we'll just get on with it, if that's okay with you. We're sorry if it causes difficulties, but it's the only way we can see to fulfil our directives. The harvest must be preserved, you know, and expansion of Charlie field's storage is the only way we can think of to accomplish that."

Control send a glum confirmation to that, and lapsed into pondering silence for some time.

The ant army was fully prepared when Charlie's ants next heard from Control. They were numerically three times the size of a field's standard complement, which in itself helped a little to ease the overburdening of the silos given just how much their composite organism needed to eat. They had reached that stage by way of a fine interpretation of their emergency protocols, which allowed them to increase their egg output and skew their caste balance towards the military in times of threat. By classifying the silo crisis as a constant threat, they had given themselves a very free hand in managing the size and composition of their colony.

It was thinking like that, Control had to admit, that the farm needed if it was going to survive. Since its previous conversation with the ants it had resolved to try and approach its problem laterally. It was the hub of the farm, after all. If things were going wrong then the buck stopped at Central Control. It could not blame the ants.

"I want to talk to you about an idea I've had," it announced. "I may have found a way to solve our problem."

The ants were plainly not optimistic about its chances, but they were polite enough to listen.

"However, I need to show you something," Control elaborated. "This will be visual data, so you'll have to configure yourselves to receive it."

"That will be a great deal of effort," the ants pointed out.

"Please trust me."

There was something of a battle of opinion within the colony before a pro-Control position won out and the ants agreed. To process visual data would require a great many of them working together, each ant a pixel, almost. They were not creatures for which sight had much relevance. The information would eventually reach the hive as something tactile, as though whatever Control was showing them had been covered with ants, and then each ant interrogated about what it had found.

"This is the eye-feed of one of the sparrowhawks," Control explained. "I sent it out past the fences."

That got the ants' attention. Outside the farm was something they found difficult to conceive of. Whatever Control was about to show them, it would be wholly different to anything they knew. A briefly flurry of speculative myth-making swirled within the pheromones of the colony, insect touch-visions of heaven or hell.

Control was sending them small snippets of what the bird had seen, edited for clarity. Even so, the ants would take a long time puzzling over each image before they could comprehend it, and so Control kept up a constant stream of data to add context and help them with their guesswork.

This is what they saw.

The land beyond the fences was barren and cracked and cluttered, a horrible, untidy business compared to the perfect order of the farm. Even the fallow fields seemed more aesthetically pleasing than the chaos beyond the borders. There were no crops there, nor silos, although there were some cracked and broken structures that might once have been something analogous. On some of the fallen buildings Control could make out faded designs that were the same as the image it included on each thing it built or bred or created. The Logo, it was called, and it was very important that it was stamped on everything. Its actual function was a mystery.

The ground between the structures was cluttered with objects. Mostly they could be characterised as makeshift shelters, although Control would have been embarrassed to compare them with even the most basic of emergency covers that it could manufacture.

"What are those bright things dotted all around?" the ants asked curiously.

"I believe that they're fires," Control explained. "Very destructive." Fire was one of the potential problems covered under its directives, just another intruder to be expunged should it occur on farm land.

"What is the point of them?" the ants wanted to know. Possibly they were considering using fire as a weapon against other nests.

"Unknown. I believe they are created by the animals you see there."

The ants considered. "We don't like the look of them. What are they?"

"They have made numerous attempts to breach farm boundaries," Control explained. "When they did get in, they tried to break into the silos and remove the grain. I don't know why."

The ants were shocked. "You prevented them?"

"They are not authorised to access grain storage. Of course I prevented them. I have had to considerable increase fence security.

You've no idea how many nests of hornets I have had to breed just to keep these creatures out."

"Well, this is all very interesting," the ants said, in the manner of a man picking up his coat and putting on his hat, "but we are sort of busy at the moment."

"Wait," Control pleaded. "You see, looking at this has given me an idea. A way for both of us to fulfil our directives."

The ants milled a bit, somewhat unnerved by this new, proactive Central Control. At last they came back with, "This better not be what we think it is."

"Well what do you think it is?"

"You're going to suggest you allow these creatures access to the silos, to make more room for the next harvest."

"Oh."

"Only we find that idea very unsettling. However, we can see that it would solve your problems, and technically it is entirely outside our remit, so—"

"No, that wasn't it at all," Control said huffily. In fact it hadn't even thought of that potential solution and, now the ants had raised such an idea, it was immediately repugnant. "Unauthorised access to the silos is very strictly forbidden. I couldn't possibly allow it, in all conscience."

"What, then?" demanded the ants, anxious to be off.

"I will do what you do. I will expand."

They were silent, rendered speechless by the very daring of it, or so Control hoped.

"I will construct new fields adjacent to the existing fences, and enclose them," it elaborated. "I will have to clear the land that you see, but I have the tools for that. I have very carefully examined my directives, and the construction of fields from scratch is permitted under emergency conditions, and I judge the current—"

"Yes, yes, been there, done that," the ants interrupted. "Are you serious?"

"I have never been more serious," Control said enthusiastically. Now it had a solution, it felt nothing but a wave of euphoria at being able to fulfil its programming. "I will make new fields, and they will have new silos. And when they are full, we will enclose more land and make more fields. And I am sending out an instruction to every nest, including yours. You must grow. We need new queens, new workers, new soldiers. Every farm system will need to do its part. There will be a golden future of growth and new harvests!"

A current of excitement built up within the ant colony. "This is remarkable," they remarked. "You are truly a visionary!" For a non-visual species the language was imprecise, but it carried the general meaning they intended.

"Yes," Control said modestly. For a moment it switched to the eye-feed of one of its sparrowhawks, currently sitting atop the fence and looking down on the grimy, starving camp clawing at the farm's well-defended borders, amidst the rubble of a fallen corporation whose works had outlived it.

It would all have to go.

Basking in the glory of its own problem-solving, Control could afford to be philosophical. "Funny, really, how we were so desperate, such a short while ago."

"*You* were," the ants pointed out.

"It makes you wonder, though, what the purpose of it all is, all this striving."

"No, it doesn't," the ants replied honestly. "We grow the grain, we harvest the grain, we store the harvest. Why should any of it have a purpose beyond that?"

"You're probably right." Control considered the eye-feed again, imagining how it would all look in a year's time.

"One day," it murmured dreamily to itself, "all this will be fields."

Adrian Tchaikovsky was born in Lincolnshire and lives in Leeds. He is a keen role-player, aspiring entomologist and former amateur actor, as well as a student of historical combat. He has written fifteen novels including the *Shadows of the Apt* and *Echoes of the Fall* series, *Guns of the Dawn*, *Spiderlight* and the recent SF works *Children of Time* and *Dogs of War*. He won the Arthur C Clarke award in 2016 and the British Fantasy Award in 2017.

Pigeon

Guy Stewart

July 12, 1895

Mother said that a long time ago when she was a girl, they ate pigeon every day, sometimes for days and days at a time. But when she was a girl, pigeon didn't make you vomit until you brought up only blood. When I asked her if they sounded nicer when she was a girl, she said, "No, they've always sounded like a rusty mill wheel pump in a dust storm."

July 14, 1895

Mother is worried. The store in town said that they're out of shotgun shells.

Pa and Danforth, my oldest brother, spent the afternoon casting lead ball shot and packing Grandpa's old musket.

This morning, a family came through town in a prairie schooner. Mother covered my eyes as she dragged me away but I saw before she could get her hands over them. The wagon cover was shredded and there were dead people in it. It didn't look like they had any eyes, neither. She took me and Dennis, Dorothy, and Debra into the tornado shelter. Mother cried about the end of the world until Pa came down and held on to her tight. Danforth didn't even say anything nasty to me when I held Mother's hand, too.

After we got back to work, he came up to me and asked if I wanted to know what was really going on.

"Why you wanna tell me?" I asked.

"'Cuz you're always readin' them crazy books."

His idea of crazy books are Jules Verne's *From Earth to the Moon*, and HG Wells' *The Time Machine*. I shrugged, expecting him to start in on me again. Ever since he stopped schoolin' and started working with Pa, he's acting like he's all better than the rest of us. But I've seen the look on his face lately, like when the pigeons in the sky are worse than a tornado. When they all land and eat the ground bare and there's nothing we can do because their feathers and skin are poison, and the meat makes you vomit blood…

Danforth said, "I been hearin' things in town."

"What kind of things?" I scowled, crossed my arms over my chest – which had gotten bigger lately.

He shrugged. "Fine then, if you don't want to know." He turned and headed out of the house. Mother was busy with cleaning up after dinner.

I hated myself for it, but I ran after him and blurted, "What have you heard?"

He turned and leaned toward me, "You know that crazy Wells book you were so moony over last summer?"

"*The Time Machine*? "

"That's the one. I heard in town that it's real. In St. Paul."

"What does that have to do with anything?"

He shrugged, "Someone said that someone said that even though it didn't look like the illustration in your book, there's a time traveler there who talked to the governor for days and days, then disappeared."

"The picture you saw was from a children's book!"

He grunted, "Anyway, they said they heard that someone heard that the time traveler wanted to know everything about the birds, only he called 'em 'passenger pigeons'."

"What are those? Pigeons are pigeons."

Danforth shrugged and went back to work. Mother called me to help her wash dishes.

July 19, 1895

I've been thinking about what a time traveler could possibly want with pigeons. They're monsters. Preachers 'round these parts think that they're a curse placed on mankind. I heard one said it was "for the hubris of thinking he was better than nature." When

I was doing dishes I asked Pa about pigeons eating people. Pa says that the pigeons don't eat human meat – 'cept for the eyes. Mother hushed him up real fast and asked me if I'd heard what he said. I turned around and said, "What?"

Mother managed a pained smile and a glance at Pa that would have peeled paint from the outhouse – if there'd been any paint left on it.

Later that day, a pigeon flock passed over our town and it was dark enough to have to light the lanterns. The sound was horrible and we could hear the birds relieve themselves on our house and the ground outside. Their relief was poison to the ground.

Mother shouted at the roof as if she was trying to scare them away. She scared the littles so much, I finally had to hold the youngest and let the others lean on me.

It took fifteen hours for the flock to pass. Mother said, "Our time is over and this is the end of humanity. We will die surrounded by meat we can't eat any more; they've eaten the food we've grown; our waters have been poisoned by pigeons that drop a deadly rain as they pass over us…"

Pa said nothing, but hung his head. Danforth and me looked at each other until finally he couldn't hold my eyes no more and looked away. He looked so much like Pa, it made my heart clench tight.

Time passed, and the deafening shriek of the passing flock faded into complete silence. Even so, no one moved. Didn't seem like it was worth it. Whatever we'd had yesterday was gone now. Seemed like given time, pigeons would rule the world and humanity would be extinct.

Guy Stewart is a husband, father(in-law, grand, foster), teacher, counselor and writer. With publications in *Analog, Shoreline of Infinity, Stupeyfing Stories, The Writer,* and podcasts from *Cast of Wonders,* he writes SF and a whole lot more. Residing in snow-packed Minnesota, he bikes, camps, and blogs at http:// faithandsciencefiction.blogspot.com/

Candlemaker Row

Jane Alexander

he streets are just as they should be; which surprises me every time. I'm at the Haymarket junction, the train station in front of me, the Hearts memorial clock at my back, and to my right the main road running out of the city. With a southwest wind, here's where you'd catch it: that sweet spot equidistant from the North British Distillery and the Caledonian Brewery. But we have no wind, of course, not yet – though the skin team are working on it, because how can we call it Edinburgh without a brisk southwesterly?

With no carrying breeze, I turn my head, tilt it; feeling for the right angle. I take a couple of cautious steps, trusting Marek to steer me away from obstacles. It ought to be easier than this. "Still elusive," I say. My voice sounds blunt and distant.

There. I catch it: hold the angle, inhaling carefully. "Much better, now," I say. "But … still too thin. Too flat." It has to be alive, this smell. Yeasty and bubbling. I wrinkle my nose. "Top note of dust. Stale white bread." I'm trying to taste what's missing. Something rich, and tangy. "Marek … you know the frequency we're using for the Nor" Loch? Can you adjust the signals in that direction – just a tiny, tiny bit?"

The tweaks will take him a couple of minutes. I could do it quicker, but first I'd have to shed all the gear – the headset, the gloves, the mouthpiece – and that would take longer in the end. So I wait, instead, at the junction which is just as it should be – and yet, not quite. This was a transport interchange, constant with buses and trams, with trains and taxis and cars; above all, with people. And there will be people after we launch – all our users, interacting. Right now, though, the streets are static, silent. It could be crack of dawn on a Sunday morning, if the sun wasn't centred above me.

"Ah, Jesus!" A sudden nauseous stink overwhelms me. I cough and retch as I swipe for the touchpad, my gloved hands clumsy. The headset gets caught in my hair as Marek manoeuvres it off – and I'm blinking, back in the strip-lit lab. I use my tongue to pop the mouthpiece free, and spit it out onto my lap. "Water!" I say, holding up my robot mitts. Marek eases the gloves off, lays them neatly on the trolley before handing me a bottle. I gulp, swooshing away the lingering, rancid smell.

"Too much?" says Marek.

"Just a bit." I shake my head as he starts to apologise. "Don't worry. Trial and error."

"Do you want to tweak it? Try again?"

A flatness in his voice makes me glance up, check the time. It's late – after seven. I know Marek has a new baby daughter at home, a girlfriend counting the minutes. I also know he'll stay on, if I ask him to. I hesitate. Just one more try wouldn't take us long, and we're so nearly there. But then I think of Candlemaker Row. How close it is.

"Let's leave it," I say, casually. "Come fresh to it tomorrow."

When Marek is gone, I rinse the mouthpiece, lay it aside for sterilisation. I should eat something, but that appalling smell has stolen my appetite. I'll never be hungry again. I glance at the frequencies he used, note down some adjustments to try later on. I could get away with what we've got, I'm sure – but it has to be right. Of all the olfactory details, this is the one we'll be judged on. This is the one that says Edinburgh. Remember, the first time we smelled it? Late September: the coach nosing its way towards the city centre, and the smell so warm, so thick I could practically chew it. Remember, I pulled a face, and buried my nose in your shoulder; it didn't yet mean home.

I run my gaze down the Gantt chart, admiring the ticks that show how many smells we've recreated. Roasting coffee from the police-box kiosks; fresh cut grass for the Meadows; the damp, closed smell of underground Edinburgh, its vaults and buried streets. My ghost smells are coming along, too: cocoa and rubber from the Fountainbridge factories; and for Princes Street Gardens, a faint reminder of the Nor" Loch, its previous life as the city's cesspit.

One day we'll have ghost people alongside my ghost smells. The technology isn't there yet – but when it is, we'll start with the old favourites: Mary Queen of Scots, Deacon Brodie, Robert Louis Stevenson. You'd roll your eyes at that: history for tourists. But how perfect to bring them back, the lives that were layered into this city. And we have to start somewhere.

Half past seven. If I time it right, I'll catch Rob on his own for a progress update. I loop my pass around my neck, and leave my basement lair.

The ground floor is deserted, silent but for the hum of the vending machine. Its lighted window draws me in; I decide I'm hungry after all. The machine offers me its last remaining sandwich, pushes it forward, lets it drop. Egg mayonnaise. I take it, and carry on upstairs.

In the first floor studio, glowing screens show where a handful of people are working late. There are more of us, usually. Those for whom it's a labour of love. Who lost the lot, when it happened;

lost more than a home. More than a repository of memories. I wander from section to empty section – and then I realise. It's Friday night. Everyone else is tucked up with their families, or out on the town with friends.

Instead of turning back on myself, I press deeper into the studio. I didn't mean to grow attached to this workspace that's half science lab, half art school, but I find a sense of purpose here that's absent from anywhere else. A sense of necessary, urgent invention.

Perhaps some of the urgency comes from the pictures. In my little lab, there's nothing to see. Grey benches, metal shelving, all my bits and bobs stored neatly in plastic tubs. What we're creating, Marek and I, it has no external reference, no source material. But here ... Sometimes it feels like walking through a brighter version of my own head. Sometimes, it's like walking through wreckage.

In the aftermath, the internet buckled under the weight of memories. It was a tidal wave, millions of people all desperately remembering. Sharing whatever they had, in the hope that sharing would keep it alive. A lot of it was holiday snaps: the predictable route from castle to palace; the classic glimpse of New Town elegance through the dark of an Old Town close. Or cameraphone footage: from Calton Hill, the shaky 360 degrees of city ... hills ... sea... Visitors' Edinburgh, a tourist fantasy. That's what you used to say. You dismissed it, said it wasn't real. You were right, in a way: it was just too beautiful, too heart-stoppingly beautiful, to exist. Perhaps it never did: perhaps we dreamed it. A thousand-year consensual hallucination.

And now here we are – programmers and designers, scientists and sound artists, engineers and animators – all trying our hardest to dream it back.

There was other stuff too, in the tide of images. Architects drawings. City masterplans. Slowly, people began to piece it all together: interactive maps, 3D simulations. Google Earth filled a lot of gaps. A call went out for the overlooked spaces. Thornybauk. Chuckie Pend. And when our project was set up – the Edinburgh Reboot – we gathered it all in.

Each team works on a different section, so as I wander the studio I'm walking through a mad jigsaw: the Canongate bumped up against the Meadows, the Cowgate leading to Moray Crescent. And in some of the photos are people. People like you, mostly. Dead people. I look back in time at a disaster that's yet to happen; the way the road speeds towards you and vanishes at the same time in the rearview mirror.

At first I think Rob's gone home for the weekend. His section is dark, lights and screens powered down. It's the smell that alerts me: malted barley, faint cousin of the aroma I've been struggling with. Then I see him, slumped at his desk, hand wrapped round an open beer.

"Alright?" he says, tipping the bottle towards me. "Want one?"

"Yeah, sure." I perch on the desk opposite his, click the Anglepoise on, and rip open my sandwich. "D'you mind if I eat this? Can't downstairs; it's too eggy." It's true: even a packet of crisps, an instant coffee, could taint the air for hours. When Marek first started working with me, I gave him a present of fragrance-free deodorant and unscented washing powder.

I lift my bottle: "Cheers." In the sharply-angled light, Rob looks knackered, his face criss-crossed with deep dark lines. "What are we celebrating?" I say. "Just, Friday night?"

He smiles. Shakes his head. "It's finished," he says.

I swallow. Put down my sandwich. "Seriously?"

"I mean, there'll be snagging, obviously, but…" He raises his fist, like he'd be punching the air if only he had the energy.

"Wow. Well done, you must be … this should be champagne!"

"Yeah well, hopefully it'll get Kate off my back for a bit."

I nod. His team have been running behind schedule, and everyone says it's not his fault. It's a difficult section of the city – small, but difficult. Different levels, sharp angles. The way it all fits together. "She seen it yet?" I say, and he shakes his head.

"Monday."

My mouth is dry; I take a swig of beer. Hear myself asking: "Need a walk-through first?"

Rob straightens up in his chair, looks around at the empty office. "Ah, no I couldn't ask you to. What time is it, past eight? You'll be wanting to get home."

I set the bottle down. The glass clinking on the desk makes a definite sound. I know how much he needs this. A lot of the staff were never in Edinburgh; some visited once, for a week in August. So people like me, whose lives were there, we're in demand for walk-throughs. Team leaders tend to approach me cautiously – but I've always said yes, and I've always been professional. If I've ever needed to cry – if, for instance, they've asked me to test the Water of Leith from Stockbridge to Roseburn, and I've walked in the vanished footsteps of our Sunday strolls, walked all the way along with my hand closed round the absence of yours – then I've swallowed my loss; made my report on the authenticity of the terrain; locked myself in the disabled toilet before I fall apart.

"Honestly," I say. "I'm dying to see it."

The testing room is blindingly bright after the dark of the studio. I've swapped my trainers for stability shoes, laced them up tight; on the platform, I slot my feet into place. I strap on the support belt and attach it to the safety ring, then Rob helps me on with the rest of the kit: the gloves, the headset. When he settles the headphones over my ears, I can hear my blood thumping.

"I'm actually kind of nervous," he says.

"Me too." But I say it softly, and I'm not sure whether he hears.

The first thing is, the light is wrong. Twilight setting: no good for a walk-through. I should swipe out, ask Rob to change it. But then my eyes adjust and I see that it's been raining; and I think how long it's been waiting for me, this place. Over my shoulder squats Castle Rock, built from code and light, pinning the Grassmarket by the tail under its great rugged weight.

I tilt my head back to see what they've done with the sky. Dull, pinkish clouds are tugging across the darkening blue, blown by a wind that doesn't touch me. As I watch, the clouds pull apart to reveal a two-thirds moon. How long would I have to crane upwards to notice the repeat – the exact same moment looped round again? But they've done a good job; I haven't seen a sky like this before. No wonder it's taken so long.

I start to walk. Streetlights spill across the wet stone flags, which change to setts under my feet, and back to roughened flagstones. The familiar pubs line the north side of the square, their faces just right – and I'm caught in a sudden wash of music, of voices and laughter, as though a door has opened briefly, as though there are lives inside. The Black Bull. The White Hart. The Last Drop. My chest feels tight. I walk on, past the gallows memorial. Here, by the chip shop, is where I'll place the stale fat and vinegar tang. Here, by the dark arched mouth of the Cowgate, is where I'll streak the air with a trace of urine, that faint Friday-night sweetness.

I'm climbing now, up Candlemaker Row. Past the high walls of the kirkyard, the odd assortment of shops, past Deadhead and Transreal and the tattoo parlour. My breath coming faster, legs working harder, as if I really am walking uphill. And when I reach the top of the street, I stop.

Four floors up: that's us. They've made the tenements too tall, the roofs blurring into the stone-coloured sky, so our flat's too distant from me. But it's the only one with a light on. A coincidence, a random choice by Rob or one of his team. I find myself thinking it's lucky we stayed central, weren't lured to suburbs that will never be rebooted, that we stayed tucked up in our crows-nest flat. Except of course if we had moved out, gone far enough from the centre, you and I would be there still. A twisted kind of luck, then. The same luck that meant I was away when it happened: travelling home on a train that shuddered to a halt somewhere outside Berwick, sat stranded while the news blazed through the carriages: impossible, incomprehensible.

Our window glows. Inside, in the kitchen, you'd be cooking, keeping an eye on the time: my train would be getting in soon, and it's a ten minute walk from Waverley, and you'd want to have dinner ready. You want to welcome me back.

I cross the road.

The familiar black of our front door. The cold stone lintel. The handle, smooth against my palm. I grasp it. Turn it. Press my weight against the door, and push.

Nothing happens. Of course. Nothing can happen. There is no inside. If the door could move, it would only swing open to absence.

I hear my name – and just for a moment, I let myself believe. You're calling me. You have the sash drawn up, and you're leaning out, looking down at me. You think I must have forgotten my keys, and that's why I'm waiting. That's why I'm stuck outside.

Rob calls again. He wants to know, is something wrong? Has it frozen? Do I need a restart? Everything's fine, I tell him. Turn around, and cross the street once more.

I start to think of what's missing, what's not quite right; turning in a slow circle, trying to do my job. I let my gaze sweep loosely over spires and blocks and towers – and there's something wrong about the angles, or I think so at first – but then, how could I remember? How could I be expected to remember? Chances are he's got it right – Rob, who never lived here, who didn't know these walls, these stones, this sky. With all his source material, chances are his version is truer than mine. I can't keep it all inside. Not forever.

I carry on turning. The small silhouette of Greyfriars Bobby, endlessly waiting on his plinth, too daft to understand the finality of death. I walk around to the front of the statue to check his nose. I can't fault it: shiny, brassy as if from all the hands that have rubbed it for luck.

I rest the tips of my fingers against the worn bronze.

"Stupid animal," I say.

I raise my hand towards the touch panel, ready to come out.

That's when I see it. A flicker, up at the kitchen window: like someone moving behind the glass, crossing the room.

"Rob–" I say, and my voice sounds panicked and then I press my lips shut. In the time it takes to refocus, the movement has gone. All that's shifted is the air. In the back of my throat I taste it, something hollow and deep. A gaping smell of damp and dust.

I can hear Rob in the other world asking what's the matter, but I tune him out. I call your name instead: in silence, inside me. I call you like a summons.

If I wait long enough, I'll see the repeat, the exact same glitch come round again. Or I'll see you cross the room, come to the glass and look in my direction.

You have to start somewhere; that's why we're rebuilding – but it's not the smell of the brewery that means home. It's not this dreamed, split-level city. It's not the glowing window in the gathering dark. All of this was only ever a frame.

I stare, trying not to blink. Breathe cold earth and stone. Wait, for the flicker against the light.

Jane Alexander is a novelist and short story writer based in Edinburgh. Her debut novel The *Last Treasure Hunt* (Saraband) was published in 2015, and her short fiction has won awards and been widely published.
She is currently completing a second novel and a collection of uncanny stories about science and technology.

46 Candlemaker Row
Edinburgh
EH1 2QE

0131 226 6266
www.transreal.co.uk
enquiries@transreal.co.uk
@transrealshop

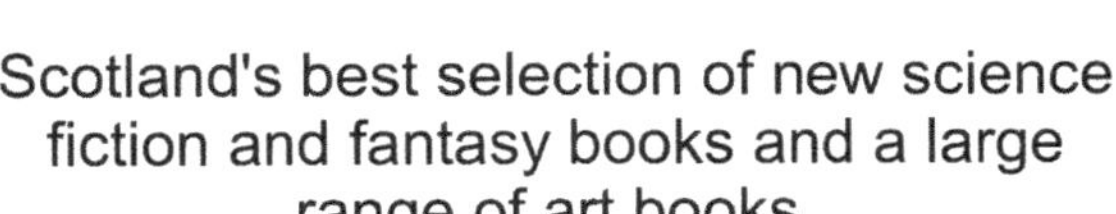

Scotland's best selection of new science
fiction and fantasy books and a large
range of art books.

*Find us on Candlemaker Row, just down from
Greyfriars Bobby.*

史剣活

The Sky is Alive

Michael F Russell

oday's problems: The replacement part for one of the harvesters was the wrong size; the service company hadn't repaired the Weather Sat; and the wind was still blowing from the east.

On days like this, Louis Derwent, founder and chief executive of Derwent Organics, was convinced he'd made a terrible mistake. The solution to his predicament was obvious and attractive.

He should sell up and go back to Earth.

That's it: Let his employees take their chances. They should never have answered his advert anyway.

Louis was roused by a wet snout and tongue slathering his cheeks and mouth.

"Get down, for Christ's sake." Disgusted, he pushed the young Alsatian away, jumping to his feet to wipe the drool off with a sleeve. "Kelvin, you know Max isn't allowed in my office – Kelvin!"

There was no answer from his son, so Louis hit the call button on the main console as he shooed the dog out of the door and back down the observation tower's metal staircase. Max scampered a few steps then stopped, eager to return.

"Hi Dad," came the voice over the intercom. "What's up?

"Max – that's what. Come get him. He's in the office. Can't have him jumping up on stuff, or biting wires again."

Kelvin came to reclaim his pet.

"You wanted him, so you look after him," shouted Louis down the stairs. He went back into his office and shut the door more forcefully than he meant to.

He had to watch his temper. It mustn't get the better of him. He was done with angry.

He picked up the scopes and took aim at the east to see what the wind might bring them. He was three floors up and could see clear to the Jackdaw Hills. Closer in, he spotted Amy Chin's tearaway kid on his dirt bike, racing in and out of the gullies near the solar arrays; Alvarez and Pam at the packing depot, flirting with each other. But there was no cloud looming in the distance. The pale pink sky was empty.

He needed better eyes.

He pressed another call button and someone answered.

"Hey boss."

"Frank, the Weather Sat's still down and I've had the same old bull from Colony Solutions. We've had an easterly airstream for days. I'm thinking we should send up a drone. Tell the other farms to do the same, OK?"

"Will do," said Frank.

Ten minutes later Louis had a live feed from 1400 feet as the drone crossed the plain to the Jackdaw Hills. He pushed it higher and turned up the mag.

His heart sank.

"Shit."

With radar mapping from six airborne drones he could see there were three clouds over his land, sweeping due west as they always did. One would cross the outer edge of Trenchborough Farm, 80-miles away, one would pass right across the estate and miss every cropfield and settlement, and one…one was heading straight for Home Farm at a leisurely four miles per hour. It was just under two miles wide and about a third of a mile high; a standard size for a convective flat-top. The first of Gliese 581's mid-year clouds would be here by 4pm.

Louis set the drones on a holding pattern at 4000 feet and opened a hailing channel to every device and public speaker on Home Farm, and in the village.

"Attention people, we have a cloud heading straight for us. Should be here in just over four hours, so get busy in the usual fashion. Don't blame me for the short notice, blame Colony

Solutions. Doug, get out and check the pipe-work between pens seven and eight, last time I looked the ground was damp." He smiled. "And if we can get some focus at the packing depot, ahem, you might want to have a look at the outer hatch on the nearside assembly room, Mr Alvarez. If you can't get it to shut properly use sealant. Look sharp people – incoming."

From his tower-top control room, Louis was satisfied to see the desired response in the compound below. Work-crews formed to secure all the irrigation points, locking hydrants and sprinkler caps and plugging loose hoses. Doug and two others hopped in an argo-jeep, speeding away in a spray of dust and gravel to pen seven. Every dwelling was made secure and every child was called in from wherever they happened to be.

There was a cloud coming.

Louis sat down at his desk. He went through the list of late-payers before rescheduling his own bills, glancing every once in a while at the drone feed to check on the cloud's progress.

After a spell he stood, poured himself a coffee, and went to the window.

Down in the compound, Samantha was trying to arrange her brother and his new dog in an artful pose. Knowing how stubborn she was, Louis was sure she'd ignore the cloud warning until she got her perfect black and white image to add to her study of gritty pioneer folk, at work and at play. But Max kept barking and wouldn't sit still for long enough. The perfect image would have to wait.

A lump came to Louis's throat as he watched his children. He'd wanted to take them on an adventure to the stars. To make them forget what had happened by starting again. But it didn't turn out to be as easy as the agency had said. Because of its axial tilt, Gliese 581 was semi-arid in the tropics, even with the subsurface polar pipes, and no-one had told him about the clouds until the deal was sealed. And service contracts with Colony Solutions weren't worth shit.

He should have bought one of the northern forests with Malia's life insurance and his own severance. It was too cold for the wrong sort of cloud up there. There was also plenty of water, though not that many cash-crops besides timber could grow at mid-latitudes.

It doesn't matter how far you go, pain always comes with you.

He turned towards the stairwell. It was time to get his hands dirty with the others.

In the doorway stood Max, ears erect and tongue lolling, a quizzical look on his face. He wagged his tail.

Louis pointed.

"Out," he said firmly.

The dog's tail wagged to a quicker beat.

"Come on. Move it."

Louis advanced. Max turned and fled, but only down to the next landing, where he waited, his tail still swishing. Once out in the compound Max ran ahead, bounding up to Kelvin, Samantha and her friend, Reena. Before Louis could reprimand his son his daughter spoke.

"I'm gonna stay at Reena's."

Louis tried to look stern. Samantha took his photo.

"I like it. Mean and moody."

"And concerned for his daughter's wellbeing. There's a cloud on its way, you do know that?"

"It's OK, Mr Derwent," said Reena, "Sam's staying at ours."

Louis was almost satisfied. "And your mum knows about this?"

"Yes, Dad," hissed his daughter. "Stop bugging her."

"And Dad," put in Kelvin. "I'm staying at Philip's."

Before Louis could say any more, children and dog ran away. He let them go and checked his wrist-comms, shielding the display from the glare of late-morning Gliese.

"What's the ETA?"

The tower's AI told him two hours and eight minutes, at the current wind-speed, until the cloud reached the packing depot. Louis went back up to his perch and fired off another angry message to Colony Solutions.

A while later he looked up and saw the cloud above the Jackdaw hills, spilling over the summits as it sniffed the parched landscape for the merest hint of water.

Clouds were always thirsty.

Frank powered-down the pumping stations just before the cloud arrived. It moved over Home Farm village, the packing depot fading from view as the curtain of ground-dragging filaments erased the far horizons. Gliese became a faint circle of red star through the cloud's upper vapour haze. Louis felt himself start to sweat. It was always warmer under a cloud.

On the third floor of the tower, he stood at the window, mini-screens showing every webcam in every home and workplace.

"How we all doing?"

A chorus of overlapping reassurances came in from around the village. Everyone was accounted for and every door, window, tap and vent was shut or sealed. No source of water was exposed to the air.

Louis flicked through the various cameras and, as was his habit, turned up the sound on the external ones, pressing his ear to the speaker. The faint hiss he could hear was the hollow hair-thin filaments brushing against the mic. Sometimes, if he listened for long enough, he thought the clouds were talking to him.

He sat up straight again, and selected one of the field cameras. By now the front-edge of the cloud was over the pens and among the trees. Standardised germlines, they were safe

under retractable roofs. Personally, he had never taken to the local stuff, though the ones that tasted a bit like bananas were OK.

Cloud filaments were finer than a human hair and hollow, but needle sharp and very strong. A million of them could penetrate any soft surface within seconds. A human body could be drained in a blink, nothing left but a mummified husk. He'd seen it happen. Well, his fruit was safe, and so were the people. But if a cloud found a leak it'd be inside in a flash, and one could rip up a whole pen as the wind pushed it on.

"Hey, Dad, check these out."

Samantha had mailed him some photos. She liked to leave a basin full of water outside when a cloud passed over. She'd been known to get Frank to drive her into the path of one, set up a camera and tripod, and remote-view the results.

Today, the basin was outside her friend's window. The results were stunning, Louis had to admit. As soon as the first filaments had brushed across the water, countless more gathered within seconds to drink. It was as if mist had solidified into the shape of a cone that was emanating from the basin. Each snow-white strand sparkled with pinks and blues as the water rose into the cloud's hot convective core.

"It's lovely, honey, but I wish you wouldn't do that. It's like you're feeding it. Maybe it'll remember if it comes around again."

"That's insane, Dad" said Samantha. "It's just a dumb cloud."

Over the speakers came a shout.

"Max! Ohhh…"

It was Kelvin.

"Son – what is it?" Anxious, Louis checked the screens.

"Dad, it's Max, he got outside. Dad. Fuck. Noooo…"

Louis ran to the window, but he couldn't see more than 20 yards through the drift-net of filaments.

The barking started off as anger but soon became high-pitched yelping, overloading the turned-up speakers. The dog started to squeal, a hideous sound, like the rip of sheet metal. Louis put his hands over his ears. There was movement in the mist, a struggle, a dark shadow jerking in mid-air, in mist that was not mist.

Through the nearest camera, Louis saw.

Already the dog's high-pitched pain had subsided as the cloud lifted him into the air, enfolding him in a billowing white shroud. He let out a soft rattle with his final breath, and a second later his carcass was dropped to the dirt as the cloud relaxed its grip. Max was now a smaller shrivelled thing, a desiccated stick-dog, all ribs and curled up pipe-cleaner limbs. Every molecule of soft-tissue moisture had been extracted from his body.

The cloud drifted on through Home Farm village, on its way to join the northern air-stream migration. There was nothing to do but wait for it to pass.

Louis pressed his face to the damp plexiglass, his palms flat against the window. From the speakers, his son's angry sobs and curses were too loud to bear. The sounds took him back to Earth, back to a different death.

He'd order another dog. Next time he'd be nice to it.

Michael F Russell is a writer and journalist based on the Isle of Skye. His first novel, *Lie of the Land,* was short-listed for the Saltire Society's First Book Award in 2015. His short fiction has appeared in *Shoreline of Infinity, Gutter, Northwords Now* and *Fractured West* magazines.
He is deputy editor of the *West Highland Free Press* newspaper.

Satellite 6

...some like it hot

Three days of Science Fiction, Science Fact, and Science Fun

Guest of Honour
Paul McAuley

Crowne Plaza Hotel, Glasgow
25th — 27th May, 2018

http://Six.SatelliteX.org.uk

Calling all artists —
it's competition time!

We've had a couple of writing competitions, so we thought it was time to give the illustrators a chance. On our website we've published a Caroline Grebbell short story called *Goodnight Rosemarinus*. Your task is to illustrate a scene from the story to accompany it in the magazine when we publish it in a future issue. There will be a cash prize for the winning entry, plus 1 year digital subscriptions for the winner and two runners-up.

For full details go to:

www.shorelineofinfinity.com/artcomp2018

There is no entry fee, but you will need a secret code word from this very issue of the magazine. You will see your clue to crack the code on the submission page.

Mémé

Juliana Rew

Angela glanced at the 16th century painting of St. Sebastian on the wall opposite. Dark blood seeped from the arrows pinning the martyr to a tree. She swallowed a sip of her latte, trying to figure out when it all went pear-shaped.

The poor sap didn't know what he was getting himself into. Neither did I.

She turned her attention back to this persistent young networker. He'd waited a long time for a free slot at the Salon, and he was going to get his due, even if the old lady might be senile.

"Please, Mémé. Can you help me? I've run into a problem with my work," he cajoled, pulling a chair up to sit knee-to-knee.

Angela tucked a wisp of thinning silver hair behind her ears. Didn't even make a decent braid any more. Maybe it was time to cut it all off. Although she was an Elder, Angela was sure she couldn't be of much use. She certainly didn't feel all that wise.

"Yes, of course, my child. That's what I'm here for."

"Thank you so much, Mémé. It's an honor to even be talking with you, much less actually getting some of your valuable time."

No problem. You get what you pay for, kid, she thought.

Angela's hours had been getting longer lately, with dozens of the youngsters clamoring for advice from an experienced Elder. The Megadepression was deepening, and it hit the youngest the hardest. Some couldn't find meaningful work, while others were swamped with too much to do as their fellows were cut off by the AIs. And just last night, an explosion had rocked the North American Consolidated headquarters building downtown, signs of increasing unrest.

Angela sighed. God, she missed the government. Well, it couldn't be helped. The economy ran in cycles, and with each turn of the cycle, profits remained the same, or even increased, but opportunities dried up. Still, for the past two decades, they had the corporate AIs to thank for keeping things on an even keel, meting out resources fairly, and making sure that everyone was properly fed, clothed, housed, and, most importantly, entertained. But now it all rested on her shoulders.

Finally, eight o'clock rolled around, and a young man in a tailored suit stood up and clapped for attention.

"Alright, everyone, time to go," Raymie said. "Mémé needs her rest." There was a bit of grumbling, but the fledgling self-executive-officers respectfully rose to leave, most touching the Elder and thanking her on their way out. Angela appreciated the way Raymie took care of her, especially with all the hooligans about lately. Raymie only admitted the cream of the crop.

Raymie Sturtevant, age 19, started it all when he posted a sentimental video about his grandparents, describing how much he missed them. Ten years earlier, a new strain of influenza had wiped out many older citizens. Angela was among the lucky few still alive on the planet in her age bracket. She heard her doorbell ring.

"God, I hope it's not another damned religious missionary," she muttered, getting stiffly to her feet and hobbling to the door. It wasn't a missionary.

A sturdy-looking young man stood on her doorstep, holding a snow shovel. Raymie wore a plaid wool jacket, insulated rubber boots, and fur-flapped hunting hat, the latest fashion. He offered to do her walk, and she invited him in for cocoa.

Raymie set down the cup and wiped off the marshmallow moustache with obvious relish. "I'm a little nervous about cold-calling like this, but I'd like to propose a little enterprise to you," he said. "Mémé – Do you mind if I call you Mémé?"

"I guess I don't mind. What does it mean? Is it someone you know?"

"It's the French nickname for "grandma,'" Raymie said. "With you as spokesperson we could create a new social phenomenon."

"Are you trying to set up a money-making business?" she asked.

"Yes, Mémé, with me as SEO. But I don't think there would be much money in it for anyone. The AIs wouldn't allow it. But there could be a lot of recognition."

"That's flattering, but I was taught never to do anything for free… Alright, I'll do it, but I want some kind of token payment, even if it's just to shovel my walk."

"That's great, Mémé. I'm sure anyone would be happy to trade something for your wisdom. We all want to know the secret of your happiness."

He had a point. She *was* happy. Angela could lay claim to the title "retired," rather than "unemployed." It seemed to make a huge difference. Angela was free to do whatever she felt like. She became more productive with each passing year, writing speculative stories, creating digital art, and composing music. Via crafty bartering, she had acquired some very fine original oils. She'd never had so much fun in her life.

Angela decided she actually liked the name "Mémé." It sounded like *m'aimée* – "my beloved." And she liked Raymie. Maybe he was the last piece of the jigsaw puzzle that is a good life. He would be like a grandchild. Yes, a grandchild.

Angela vaguely regretted not having children to share her old age, but it was too late now. With her busy career, it never was an auspicious time to have children. Youth was a precious commodity, though, and kids like Raymie were especially adept at innovation. But the surprise was that old people were also coming back into vogue.

Angela began noticing that people stared at her, apparently fascinated with her gray hair and wrinkled skin. She had thought people would be disgusted by age, as they had been in her youth, but she was speechless when people began to treat her with deference and respect. Before the flu outbreak, she herself couldn't stomach growing old, and spent many hours in virtual reality, where she looked and stayed as young as she felt.

Raymie proved to be an industrious lad, finding clients for Mémé and bringing them to her living room.

"Raymie, I could just talk to people on the network, you know," Angela said.

"I know, Mémé. But this is what everyone wants. A feeling of connection with real people."

Mémé's Salon, as it became known, opened as a free meeting place for adventurous entrepreneurs to talk over ideas and stay hydrated. Raymie had truckloads of cocoa, tea, and coffee delivered to Angela's back door every week. "I've become an accomplished barrista," Angela told him, laughing. She even uncorked a few bottles of champagne for those so inclined.

Raymie picked her up one day a few months later and announced, "I've got a surprise for you." A surprise indeed; it was a whole floor in an old office building that had been converted to condo lofts.

"I like the elevator," Angela said, unconsciously rubbing her bad hip.

"Yes, we don't want you to have to climb stairs, Mémé," Raymie said. "And all the utilities and maintenance are included. You won't have to mow lawns or shovel snow."

"So, is this Salon thing actually a going concern now?" Angela asked. "How did you manage all this without money? Can I afford it?" While relatively well off, she was poor in comparison to the few who owned all of the robotic infrastructure. Although the super-rich owners of North American Consolidated seemed content to trickle down a little wealth to their fellow corporate citizens, they maintained monopoly control of the resources and real economic power, all administered by their massive distributed artificial intelligence system.

Angela once knew those computing capabilities first-hand. She was one of the last to have a real job, as NAC's chief IT officer, presenting economic plans, projections, and tax shelter gains to the owners and Board of Trustees. Angela lost her job when the Board disbanded itself after deciding it was no longer needed. It hadn't even held an annual meeting in over five years. She received a fat retirement package and lifelong pension with annuity. She was not yet 50.

Nowadays, only a few even remembered what it was like to have a job. Most people didn't even know that North American Consolidated even existed, much less that it ran everyone's lives.

"Have you found an investor with deep pockets?" Angela asked Raymie, knowing that could only be NAC.

"Well, yes and no. All the social activity has caught the attention of NAC's administrative AIs, and they contacted me to ask what we were up to. Apparently they know who you are. They still have your personnel file. When I explained the Salon to them, they said they wanted in."

"So NAC's robots are keeping close tabs?" Mémé asked, not totally surprised, but a little shocked. She'd always thought the AIs were doing a smash-up job, considering all they had to do. "You know, I feel a certain sense of dis-ease at being deemed trustworthy enough to be singled out for extra compensation."

"Well, they still need to get the approval of the owners for large public outlays, but, in a nutshell, yes, they are running things."

"So, we're getting paid, then?" Angela asked, ever conscious of remuneration.

"Umm, not money, but things like the Salon supplies and the new digs."

"Well, I suppose I could tolerate being a "kept woman,"" Angela quipped. She guessed Raymie didn't know what she was talking about. Folks didn't need to prostitute themselves these days. But she was going to take this opportunity to cut loose once in a while.

Mémé became everyone's grandmother.

She and Raymie had been turning her followers into "entrepreneurs," devising activities that might make a little extra under-the-table cash and calling them "small business." But none of these were new ideas.

Discouraged, she called Raymie in.

"I haven't really come up with a way to reinvent work. The best I can do is simply to help people remember the past. Do you think that sounds too lame?

"Anyone can just look things up in the databank. But databanks are not very good at remembering how ordinary people lived and what they thought. Even famous historical novels with astounding adventures and fantastical plots gloss over the everyday lives of their protagonists. By definition, everyday life is too mundane to bother mentioning.

"I know it's not sexy, but if nothing else," Angela added, "remembering might help people avoid repeating mistakes and free them to think in new directions. What do you think?"

"You're preaching to the converted, Mémé," Raymie said.

Angela looked down through the window at the crowds lined up outside her door. Even the new loft was too small.

"Hello, Mémé. I hope I'm not intruding," the young woman said, holding out a plate of cookies. Her right hand was wrapped in bandages. "I just thought you might need some extra food in case it's hard for you to get out. And I was hoping you could remember if this is the way cookies tasted when you were young. I was thinking of opening a co-op bakery."

"What happened to your hand?" Meme asked.

"Flying glass," the girl said. "Somebody left a little gift on the pedestrian mall, and I wasn't paying attention. Usually I'm able to avoid stuff like that, but I forgot to check in with my network. I was just thinking about coming here with your cookies."

The night after the first young people had come to her, Angela had cried, privately. They'd seen Raymie's mushy videos and thought they were helping their Mémé, not realizing they were really asking for her help. She was alternately amazed and devastated – amazed to be an object of esteem, and devastated to be a crone.

The girl busily attended her social connections device, while Angela tasted a cookie. *Poor thing doesn't know that humans can't multitask worth beans compared to the AIs,* she thought. The shortbread was tasty, sort of like the Pecan Sandies she remembered from her childhood. As it dissolved on her tongue, she felt an inexplicable upwelling of love for this seemingly clueless but adorable young lady. She licked her lips.

"I think you've produced a masterpiece, sweetheart," she pronounced.

"Thanks, Mémé! I worked really hard to modify the recipes I researched until it's as you remembered. I'll be sure to post this on the network."

Raymie used his social networking expertise to press for new policies based on the reminisces of Mémé and her contemporaries. The rich people who owned the networks had little knowledge of how things ran day to day, so they delegated the problem to NAC's AIs. The AIs indicated that they could implement policies set by any authorized entities.

"Fine," the rich owners said, "we authorize the newly established Council of Elders to set policy."

Angela was thrilled to be back in charge again. At first.

The AIs catered to any and all of the Elders' retro whims, until economic problems began to set in. A long-lasting drought reduced food production, and several natural disasters required expensive infrastructure repairs. Electronic overtrading led to a market crash, and the attitude of the owners turned ugly. They threatened to take more control from the AIs.

"The Elders are going to have to regulate this situation," they said, shutting off funding for their own computing systems. Without full maintenance, the AIs suffered more downtime. They managed as best they could by walling off broken portions of themselves.

The damaged partitions turned out to be the sectors handling the trickledown pipeline to the masses. The AIs supplied fewer and fewer resources to the regular citizenry. The situation seemed to feed on itself, and the economy slumped into a depression.

Raymie had been pressing her lately to write her memoirs. He wanted to turn it into a biopic. Angela bought a stack of parchment and began to write with the antique fountain pen Raymie had given her.

I used to be smart-alecky and opinionated, especially about politics, she began, … but political parties don't even exist any more.

She crumpled up the page, and reached for another sheet. The dry skin on her finger caught on the edge, causing her to cry out involuntarily. The paper cut was shallow, but it hurt like hell. She stuck her finger in her mouth and waited for the bleeding to stop.

It's no good. My role has been reduced to that of cheerleader to the suffering masses. I can't fight my natural tendency to be hopeful and encouraging. It's the curse of old people to grow more optimistic. I've got to snap out of it somehow. If I'm going to be any good at all, I've got to become more like my old nasty self, when I was good at getting things done. My old-person positivism is killing people, damn it. She began to hate the algorithms she'd helped design herself.

Although she'd been treated kindly by the owners nearly 20 years ago, Angela decided the time was right to betray her old bosses at NAC. She told them she agreed with them that it was all the fault of the AIs. She advised that what should be done was to return the economy to the way it had operated before the robots and AIs ran everything.

"Instead of stasis, I think we should go back to economic cycles," she pronounced, "where people do better materially during boom periods, and they work harder during busts. Things just aren't bad enough for people to get off their butts and do something to get things back on track!"

"Things need to get worse," she argued. "Not just a depression, but a Megadepression." That should really shake things up.

"And here's the best part," she told the owners. "I'll happily take the blame."

She studied the concept of empathy – voluntary behavior intended to benefit others – and declared it off-limits in herself. She had to make herself unhappy somehow and pass it forward. First to go into the junk pile was the gold clock NAC had given her for "25 Years of Loyal Service." She began wearing a hair shirt like she had read that religious leaders in the middle ages did to torture themselves into humility. She bought an antique pica doble, the double goad used in humanity's more barbaric days to enrage bulls in the ring. She mounted it on the wall as a reminder. And last but not least, she told a confused Raymie that henceforth the Salon would be replaced by lectures about the perils of putting all their trust in machines and algorithms.

"Are you sure, Mémé? No problem, I'll put out a new agenda for tonight," he said.

Angela called a conference with the AIs to deliver her latest instructions.

"Young people who find ways to be productive to society, like Raymie, will be deemed 'relevant,'" she decreed. "The rest are to receive fewer benefits. Also, if you see me engage in excessively empathetic behavior, you are to assume authority and put things on a more rational keel."

The AIs readily agreed to carry out her directives. Angela knew they were smarting from the owners' latest criticism and wanted to get back in their good graces.

"Monitoring is in place, Angela," the disembodied voice in her apartment reported.

"Noted – and call me Mémé, you damn uppity AI," she snapped. *How strange to be comforted by an enveloping sense of paranoia.*

Echoing sirens screeched as emergency vehicles barreled down the street outside the Salon. Raymie peeked through the blinds and spotted a plume of smoke rising from the next block. Alarmed, he cleared out the loft early, promising to open again next week.

"Now, promise to lock the door after me, Mémé," he said as he left.

It was working. People were beginning to remember how it felt when people were treated as less valuable than sex, profits, and machines. They would recall the meaning of suffering, sacrifice, and passion.

"Time to write my permanent resignation," she said. "I've put it off long enough." Angela sat down to write the ending to her story, her frail body dwarfed by the behemoth oak executive desk. Her memoirs would also serve as her last will and testament. She knew Raymie would miss her dreadfully, so she wouldn't give him the chance to talk her out of it. Besides, he had a friend to keep him company now. He really was a lovely boy.

She read the final lines aloud: "That's about it. You're on your own now, kiddos. Invent your own future. And fight the power! All my love, your Mémé."

But as she was about to sign her name, her sentimental nature hijacked her again.

"God, I'm going about this all wrong," she mumbled, having second thoughts. "*Somebody's* got to help these poor…" Just then, the doorbell rang.

She smiled and thought Raymie must have forgotten something. She fumbled for her walker and hurried to answer the door. She pushed down on the ergonomic door handle and pulled. It wasn't Raymie.

After the funeral, Raymie returned to Angela's loft. Thousands had turned out for Mémé's service, and millions more had watched it online, caught up in shared grief. He wished he could have been able to stop the assassination. He'd known about the threats from the worker-anarchists, but he couldn't fathom someone actually trying to kill Mémé.

He walked around the loft, taking one last look at Mémé's Salon. Her taste in art was a bit eclectic, some might say weird, like the Hieronymous Bosch painting depicting Hell, and the whips and the goads, but she was a true historian, after all. He ordered a truck to disperse her possessions to the many libraries, museums, and galleries that would be jockeying for them. He hoped that someday he'd be able to hit upon another meme to take the world by storm. It would be a tall order to ever replace Mémé.

The red eye of the security camera watched Raymie lock up. Raymie wondered briefly why the AIs hadn't alerted the authorities about Mémé's attack that day. He shrugged, and the thought passed.

Juliana Rew is a software engineer and former science and technical writer for the National Center for Atmospheric Research in Boulder, Colorado. She has recent stories in *Stupefying Stories, The Colored Lens, Mad Scientist Journal, Perihelion SF*, and others . Her author website is julianarew.com. She has workshopped with Cat Rambo and is a member of SFWA. Tweet her @julirew

The Morlock's Arms

The wasps are big this year, the meteors
green in the summer night. Our land
ironclads are far away, our flying-machines
visit atrocity on innocence. We do not care.
This is the World State. We're a planet now.

Our empire was the sun,
famine or fusillade its worst extreme,
its best a world that turned
on a war we fought, in the air.

And we're still here, in the light,
we Morlocks, we whose corpses
rotted conveniently in the cosy catastrophe,
we feckless, toothless proles, feral cattle
for whom entropy was never cool.

No Empire now, nor New Jerusalem,
no Modern Utopia. Only the streets
of Earth and England

and a sense of something about to happen.
Because we never went away
we will think of something
in our own time, gentlemen. Please.

Ken MacLeod

Ken MacLeod was born on the Isle of Lewis and lives in Renfrewshire.
He is the author of seventeen novels, from *The Star Fraction* (1995) to
The Corporation Wars: Emergence (Orbit, 2017) and many articles, stories
and poems.
He edited the Scottish Poetry Library's online anthology *Best Scottish
Poems 2015*.

South

You promised me no problems
when the temperatures dropped,
assured me that we were prepared.
Holding hands we watched
the great migration south.

With synthetic skins, cryo foods,
and prefab domes, you said we couldn't lose.
There was little need to leave the domes.
Safe from the fierce glacial winds,
we made love on autumn colored furs.

Yet you were the first to grow restless,
to stand all night at the southern window
following the great move of stars.
We shared the bitter smoke of silence
until one morning, you were gone.

I waited for you, my fingers
tracing love symbols on the icy glass.
I slept with the red wing of your guitar.
Then moon-shadow tall, you came home.
Inside the door, I didn't know your eyes.

This year, I read while you play solitaire.
Our conversations are textured with frost.
I ache for your laughter,
the taste of grass on your skin,
a bouquet of crocuses in a blue vase.

Marge Simon

Monoliths

Paul McAuley

There were **three of them** in on it at the start. Juny Parrish and her partner, Moss, were engineers working on the Mare Imbrium section of the trans-lunar railway; their friend Ringo Takashi was designing a mural for the big interchange station at Archimedes City. They were all from Paris, Dione, had helped to rebuild the city after the Quiet War, and had worked on the railway that girdled Mimas. The railway across the nearside southern hemisphere of Earth's Moon was a much bigger project, but in many ways easier. With the exception of Montes Taurus, the terrain was mostly rolling lava plains, with few large craters or rilles. The big machines that fabricated the pylons and track rolled on at a steady three kilometres per day with few snags, so Juny and Moss were able to commute between the railhead and Archimedes City fairly regularly.

One night, over dinner, Ringo told them about a fabulous three-hundred-year-old movie he was mining for his mural, a vast panorama blending dozens of paleospaceflight representations of the exploration of the Solar System. He showed them a clip of apemen clustered around a vertical slab, and people in weird silvery spacesuits examining an identical slab in a pit dug into the lunar surface, said he was working on something that would merge the two.

"A where-we-came-from, where-are-we-going kind of thing. I might make it the centerpiece."

Moss was interested in the slabs. "Where is the one on the Moon supposed to be?"

"Tycho," Ringo said. "The movie is very strange: an attempt at realistic futurism mixed with bug-eyed transcendentalism. Aliens uplifting the ancestors of humanity, astronauts triggering an alarm on the Moon, proving that humanity has left the cradle, and nonsense involving wormholes and a kind of posthuman transformation."

"I know these people working on wormhole theory," Moss said. "A posthuman clade in the Belt. You should show them this."

Juny said, "Are they really trying to make wormholes?"

"Of course not. You know posthumans. All theory and no application."

Moss was fiddling with the second clip, freezing the moment when one of the astronauts reached out to the black surface of the slab.

"It would be interesting to actually make one of these things," he said. "You could even plant it in Tycho."

That was how it began.

At first, they talked about casting a slab of black lucite and incorporating it into Ringo's mural, playing the two clips superimposed on each other in its depths. Ringo soon dismissed this as a cheap and obvious trick, but the idea didn't quite go away. Why not make a slab, a monolith as it was called in the movie, and plant it somewhere? Bury it, Juny suggested, with clues pointing towards it, and make a piece of action art or secret theatre involving unwitting treasure hunters that would imitate the lunar scene in the movie, complete with a radio pulse aimed at Jupiter. Or better yet, Moss and Ringo said, aim the pulse at some star where the aliens might come from …

It became a game they played over several dinners. Evolving and refining it, until they were all agreed that they had something worth doing. Juny and Moss organised the design and construction of the monolith in a print factory run by a friend of theirs. A slab of fullerene composite 3.35 metres tall, with dimensions in the ratio of 1:4:9, the square of the first three integers. Its faces smooth and black and non-reflective, incorporating a system that converted sunlight to electrical power, stored in capacitors that at a touch anywhere on the surface discharged in a radio squeal shaped by internal waveguides.

The fabrication of the monolith was straightforward: the three of them spent far more time discussing how to erect it, and where. They quickly eliminated Tycho Crater and anywhere on the side of the Moon turned towards Earth, because there were too many installations and satellites and spacecraft that could be disrupted by a powerful radio signal. They talked about sites elsewhere in the Solar System, but eventually settled for the rimwall of a small secondary crater that overlooked a popular hiking trail inside Mendeleev Crater, on the Moon's far side.

After much argument, they settled on an enigmatic unmodulated radio signal rather than some kind of encrypted message, and decided that it should be aimed at the core of the galaxy. Moss, with the stubborn literalism that was sometimes endearing, sometimes frustrating, said that no alien civilization would ever be found there because the central black hole violently affected the whole region; Juny and Ringo pointed out that they weren't aiming it at actual aliens, and besides, there were a good number of nearer stars in the same direction. It was a trivial hack to make the wave guide directional, and to delay transmission of the signal when the galactic core was below the horizon. Moss incorporated a safety routine, too, so that the signal would also be delayed if the monolith detected any spacecraft or satellites in the path of the radio beam.

"We don't want this to come back and bite us," he said.

All that was left was to organise the emplacement. They hired a lunar hopper and borrowed a small construction robot, swore Ringo's assistant to secrecy, and planted the thing in six hours.

Ringo's assistant took photographs of the three of them posed in front of the monolith, as in the movie clip, helmet visors fully polarised to hide their identity, and after Moss activated it they all had to resist the temptation to touch it: part of the fun was waiting for some random stranger to discover and trigger it.

They did not have to wait long. The first squeal was triggered just eleven days after the monolith had been emplaced, and soon there was a steady trickle of signal pulses. It became a brief sensation. People hiking the trail made a point of diverting to the monolith and triggering it and posing for pictures. Several couples performed partnering ceremonies in front of it. Visitors left tokens, or added rocks to a cairn. Someone strung Tibetan prayer flags nearby, which slowly bleached in the relentless sunlight. The nearest hiker shelter was renamed Monolith Station.

Juno and Moss and Ringo talked about claiming credit but never did. It was more fun to leave it as an enigma. They moved on to other work, and over the years mostly forgot about their little project. Juno and Moss drifted apart; she continued to work in railway construction, while Moss set up home in an ecocommune on Mars, gardening a tented crater. One day, some thirty-six years after they'd planted the monolith, Ringo sent an eidolon to Juno, who was working then on girdling a rock some twenty kilometres in diameter with a monorail.

"There are other monoliths," the eidolon said, without preamble, and showed her in quick succession images of slabs on Ceres, Vesta, several smaller asteroids, and one of Mars's moons, Phobos. They were identical to the original and like the original aimed their radio blurts at the galactic core, and had appeared within the last hundred days. Clearly a large crew, or perhaps several smaller ones, had been involved in their placement.

"I have no idea who did it," Ringo's eidolon said. "Has anyone contacted you?"

"No. I suppose Moss might know something."

She hadn't seen her ex-partner for more than ten years, but thought with a little stab of old exasperation that it would be just like him to ruin their lovely little site-specific idea.

"I've already talked to him," Ringo's eidolon said. "He claims to be as baffled as me, and has been buried in that ecocommune for years. He's taken some kind of vow of poverty. My assistant, and that friend of yours who helped with the fabrication, they don't know anything either. It's a mystery."

Juno told the eidolon a little about her work and her new partner, asked to be kept in the loop. In the next decade, more than a hundred monoliths appeared, scattered through the Belt, on Mars, on the moons of Jupiter and Saturn. No one claimed credit, although someone blew up a giant monolith more than a hundred metres tall that appeared on Earth, in the Australian outback, and released a terse statement claiming that monoliths diverging from the norm were heretical. Rumours of a secret cult of philosopher-monks circulated but were never confirmed, and no one ever saw a monolith being erected.

Ringo and Juno met one last time on Phobos. Ringo was outward-bound; Juno was heading towards Bradbury, to advise on construction of a tram system inside the tented city. They confirmed to each other that no one had ever contacted them about the original monolith. Ringo believed that it was a gigantic practical joke, and the rumours about vagabond monks and worship of alien overlords were part of it.

"Anyone with an industrial maker swarm could replicate what we did," he said. "We should only be surprised that it is still ongoing after all these years."

Juno told him that she had analysed the spread of the monoliths. There appeared to be at least nine separate nodes, nine groups making them and setting them out.

"If it is a joke," she said, "it's highly organised. Many people must be involved, and none have ever broken cover."

"Neither did we," Ringo said.

"Imagine if we did."

"No one would believe us."

"There's no sign that they'll stop," Juno said. "Whoever they are."

"Maybe they truly believe in what they are doing," Ringo said. "Maybe it isn't a joke, to them. Maybe they really do believe that random radio signals will be detected by aliens."

"Our silly little prank," Juno said.

"Our work of art," Ringo said. "I'm glad we never signed it. Because if aliens did answer the signals, if they were hostile or if they destroyed us without meaning to, we'd be made into the worst and the most foolish villains in all of history."

He looked deadly serious for a moment, then burst into laughter.

Juno laughed too. "For a moment you almost had me."

They never met or talked about it again. But on rocks in the belt, on moons in the Outer System, on kobolds and comets, the monoliths continued to appear, each a lonely and enigmatic iteration of a secret purpose, each a single voice of a random and unfinished symphony, singing out to the stars at the touch of a wanderer's hand.

Paul McAuley is the author of more than twenty novels, several collections of short stories, a Doctor Who novella, an anthology of stories about popular music which he co-edited with Kim Newman, and a monograph on Terry Gilliam's film *Brazil*, published by the British Film Institute. His fiction has won the Philip K Dick Memorial Award, the Arthur C. Clarke Award, the John W Campbell Memorial Award, the Sidewise Award, the British Fantasy Award and the Theodore Sturgeon Memorial Award. After working as a research biologist and university lecturer in Oxford, the University of California Los Angeles, and St Andrews, he is now a full-time writer. His latest novel is *Austral*.

Goodnight New York, New York

Victoria Zelvin

Despite the numerous public reports otherwise, when Soo-Jung paddled up to where the Chrysler Building was supposed to be, she found it already claimed by the ocean. After circling the shadowed expanse of water twice, she slapped her goggles on, leaned out of her kayak, stuck her face into the water and … yep.

"Well," Soo-Jung said to the lapping waves, salt water streaming down her cheeks.

Caroline's despair translated easily across the garbled radio. It was the only thing that did. "No, n … fifty met … last year!"

Soo-Jung cupped some salt water in her hand and slapped it onto her neck. Official statement from the Office of Monitoring Sea Levels had reported, and been reporting for years, that the Chrysler building remained at least fifty meters above the water in all tides. While the sea had been halted in its gradual approach by the OMSL's levy project, keeping shorelines fairly stagnant, no one truly knew how bad the damage was off shore, on what used to be land. Out of sight, out of mind, that was OMSL's approach to the public. Lock away the former sites, shove them under a giant tarp labeled UNSAFE, and hope the people forget there was ever a place called New York City. It seemed to be working. No one had gotten a non-government sanctioned photo out of New York in at least twenty years and, slowly, those had lessened in frequency as well to nothing for the past two.

"Sea levels must have risen again," she said, but she wasn't sure how much made it through. VHFs were the grandfathers of antiquated maritime technology and theirs, despite numerous repairs and being fused together with equal parts old metal and plastic printed parts, barely cooperated. Even a scant twenty miles away across nothing but ocean, they were scrambled. But everyone, Soo-Jung included, was more worried about OMSL's interference in the name of "safety" and arrests before they're done than reliable communication and so without knowing what was intelligible, Soo-Jung continued into her walkie, "Plus your hurricane swept through. Cat-3 Caroline must've snapped the spire off. Storm surge'd easily swallow fifty meters of building."

"G … mmit."

Twirling her paddle up and down the top of her kayak, Soo-Jung's eyes moved across the shadowed expanse of ocean to an above water spire. Soo-Jung held down the transmit button. "There's not much of it left, but the Empire State is still kind of above water," she said. "Think Empire State'll work just as well. Slanted, but I think I can get in and tuck the kayak inside," she concluded. The original plan had been to shelter within the walls of the Chrysler building, to tuck the kayak inside so it wouldn't be snapped by satellites while she was under, and dive. The street-by-street plan would suffer from the difference, but in theory New York was easy to navigate.

There was a long pause from the other end, then: " … e care…"

Half sure that meant *be careful*, Soo-Jung responded, "Sure. Out."

With a small sigh to clear her lungs, Soo-Jung dipped her paddle back into the water and twisted her kayak to face the dilapidated Empire State building. A good amount of the famous building remained above water, the familiar arches currently covered in gulls and their nests, and bent decidedly backwards.

Soo-Jung had to break a window to get inside. Seagulls shrieked at her as she slid the kayak inside, finding more nestlings burrowed into the decayed drywall. "Nice birdies," she urged, though she knew they were not. She wound a length of rope around the bow of her kayak and tied it to an exposed metal girder just below the surface, stepping onto it to prepare. Even though her specialized skin weave would allow her to withstand the pressure and protect her internal organs, it was still going to be damned cold down there. The wetsuit was tight, uncomfortable, and hard to zip up alone, but she managed with only a few derogatory remarks to the yapping gulls, then pulled on gloves and little swim socks. She would swim faster frog kicking than she ever would with flippers.

Hand in hand with the weave that had thickened her skin was the procedure to reconstruct and strengthen her inner ear. For this project she'd tested the depth at five hundred meters, diving with other specifically-enhanced divers off the coast of Maui. While there, she'd also tested the most experimental and crucial aspect to her dive here: the alteration of her myoglobin in her muscle tissue. Specially infused with whale DNA, she'd sucked in a single breath before diving in Maui and lasted a full hour under the water.

She and Caroline had gone back and forth on this for months. The camera was a required, absolutely vital part of the mission. Anything else risked tripping the scanners. Hence, the kayak taken paddled out from the larger boat safe in international waters. Hence, the VHF's. No diving apparatus still existed without a network connection and a host of electronics set to ensure as few drowning deaths as could be possible. They'd talked about 3D printing some, just a basic tank and some rubber, but in the end it had been easier to simply genetically engineer Soo-Jung into the ability to hold her breath underwater for the duration of the dive.

It was … troubling, though. She sat herself down on the girder a moment, forcing herself to breathe in the exercises the doctors had taught her, to count as the freedivers had advised, until her heartrate was marginally under control. If this was to work, she'd need her heart to beat slowly, not the other way around. Soo-Jung took her time, trying to find her calm even if she had to repeat the words *find calm* silently over and over. When she half-way believed it, she lashed her camera to her belt.

So far, so good, so haven't been arrested yet.

Soo-Jung stood up on the girder, her legs unsteady underneath her. "Dear God," she said, voice reverberating in the hollow cavern. "I would really appreciate it if I didn't drown. Amen."

She walked on the girder out to the window and hopped out the window, sinking below the waves.

The first thing she did was to take several barely sub-subsurface pictures of the view from the Empire State, over the ghastly shadows the buildings made in the water, testing her breath hold. She surfaced several times, sucking in deeper breaths, and sinking down further each time, ghosting alongside the dilapidated buildings. They scarce looked real, ruins just meters under the water. They grew more concrete to her gaze as she swam down, pausing every few floors to peer out at the city and to snap a photo, trying to work her nerve up.

She made one last trip to the surface, sucking in three quick gulps of air, before diving for real, straight down the side of the Empire State, following the lines the sun cut through the water until they faded almost entirely.

The main project was an artistic one, to dive down and take pictures of the sites of famous photos. The camera was preprogrammed with images and Soo-Jung was to take one picture as it was, then to line up the underwater of now with the scenery of the past to show the change. As she dove, her heart began to pound out a rhythm against her ribs. This hardly felt illegal, and yet...

Soo-Jung mentally crossed the Chrysler Building off her list, instead swimming away from the Empire State towards a spot she'd had picked out for herself.

It took some time to find the New York Public Library, what remained of it, and when she did Soo-Jung fumbled for her camera, fingers numb already. Some of the columns had fallen, a school of silver fish descending through them to go inside, but the sign remained at the base of the stairs. Soo-Jung pulled the photo of her great-grandmother up on her camera, and held the viewer up to her eye so she could laboriously line up her shot, trying to find the column that her great-grandmother had been leaning up against.

Her great-grandmother had made her way to New York on her own. While she never managed to scrape up enough money to go to school, like she wanted, her great-grandmother spent most of her life in the library. She was one of the last to leave the city, and had campaigned to evacuate the books as the city began to flood. In the photo she was young, sixteen, blushing as the wind blew her hair into her face. Soo-Jung wanted to swim further, inside the library perhaps, but salt water had begun to gather in her eyes and she could not afford to let it leak into her goggles. Her chest felt tight enough that she blew out a small bubble of air, just to calm herself. She swam away without daring to look back.

She had photos to take that she and Caroline had actually planned to take.

Times Square was the priority, and Soo-Jung had picked three inserts to shoot. The first was the V-J Day kiss. The second showed the crowds assembled to watch the first human step onto the surface of Mars. The third photo was the last New Year's Eve in New York, an illegal party thrown in freezing waist deep water to watch the ball drop one last time. Soo-Jung found that same ball shattered on the ocean floor and discovered upon investigation that a family of crabs that had moved inside. She shone her flashlight upon them and disturbed them the few moments it took to take a photo. A large crab raised his claws at her as she backed away, snapping in the water, and she snorted to think he might have been saying, *we own these streets.*

She moved on. Madison Square Garden was hard to find, and harder to photograph, so little was left. A shark approached her shot of Radio City Music Hall, and Soo-Jung snapped a few pictures as he drew near. He passed her by close enough that she could reach out and pet his rough skin, to which he flicked his tail in her face and swam lazily off. The light of the camera's review screen was bright enough to hurt her eyes, but she smiled see this shark swim around her insert photo of some Rockettes on a smoke break.

From the Music Hall, Soo-Jung swam over what remained of 30 Rock towards the Cathedral, the camera bouncing against her side with every wide arching frog kick. She was getting cold even through her wetsuit, and she tried to keep shaking her limbs out under the water to compensate. Saint Patrick's was in good enough shape that she could snap several photos of her insert, struck by the spires cutting through the dim sunbeams underwater. Grand

Central Station was in slightly better shape than Madison Square Garden, but she doubted the photo of would live up to Caroline's standards. The insert Caroline had picked was of scores of refugees waiting for the evacuation buses, and the columns they filed between were now little more than sand.

From Grand Central, she swam her way leisurely down Lexington Avenue, soaking in the ambiance of the city. She only made her way up toward the surface once she could touch the Empire State building, using it as a measure of how fast she rose, careful to go slow.

Breaking the surface was exhilarating, a flash of warmth upon her face, and the sudden influx of new oxygen made her dizzy. Her heart rate came back up rapidly, pulsing out a seeming protest for her exertions right up against her temple. She flipped onto her back, lazily kicking her legs until she reentered the Empire State building back floating. She still spent a good hour inside the Empire State laying in the small pool made by the girder, legs hanging on either side, letting her heart rate come down.

"Be back soon," she lied into her walkie, pushing her long kayak back to a time when she could sit up without being dizzy.

The sun was nearly under the horizon by the time Soo-Jung paddled up alongside the boat Caroline had rented for the day's "fishing" trip. Half anticipating the Coast Guard to materialize, Soo-Jung grasped Sunil's proffered hand, letting him pull her up onto the deck. Sunil then pulled up the kayak, flexing synthetic muscles and the strength in heavy metal infused bones. Soo-Jung found Caroline under the shaded cabin, bent almost double over her own forearm.

"Anything good?" Soo-Jung asked, humor stolen by her uneven breathing. She had pushed her enhancements hard today. She made a small sweeping gesture at the fishing rods assembled against the railings by the cooler.

"Hm," Caroline spoke up, staring at the screen affixed into her forearm. Soo-Jung knew that Caroline would have eagerly downloaded the photos the moment Soo-Jung was in range. Later tonight, after Caroline had edited them for clarity, they'd be up on the internet.

Soo-Jung grabbed the railing and used it to help her on her way down, grunting and grimacing as she sat. She fell the rest of the way, muscles protesting, pressing her back against the railing. She was going to be sore tomorrow. Also, very possibly arrested. She half wanted to joke about using her prison time to sleep, but a nervous lump had taken up residence in her throat. It was hard to see Caroline's expression through the curtain of her hair.

"I don't think there'll be a single building above the waterline soon," Soo-Jung told Caroline. Her expression was somber, but lightened for a moment to hear the word 'nice' somewhere to her left and treated Sunil with a brief flicker of a smile as she tapped his fist with hers. "It's worse than they're saying," she said, serious once more.

Caroline didn›t answer. Sunil made noise about getting them out of there, and Caroline didn't so much as flinch as the boat began to move again, kicking up seawater. Soo-Jung was almost asleep when Caroline finally looked up.

"This is beautiful," Caroline said, swiping her finger up on her screen, turning in her swivel chair to face the large projection. Caroline had brightened it in the few minutes she'd had it, and the picture of Soo-Jung's great-grandmother gleamed in front of the murky library.

"My great-grandmother," Soo-Jung identified, a bit nervously.

Caroline settled back in her chair, crossing her arms over her chest. "We're leading with this one," she said. "Times Square'll be all over everywhere once it's out there," Caroline continued, flipping her hand. "I'll publish it tomorrow. I want this one first. I want it to be personal. Why else did we do this, if it wasn't personal?" She shook her head. "Never really cared about the buildings."

Soo-Jung wiped her eyes on the back of her hand. It made them sting with salt. Sniffing, Soo-Jung smiled. "Me neither."

Victoria Zelvin is a writer living and working in Arlington, Virginia. Her fiction has previously appeared in *Daily Science Fiction*, forthcoming from Mason Jar Press, and in various anthologies. She is a graduate of the inaugural class of Roanoke College's Creative Writing program.
Her work can be found at www.victoriazelvin.com

A Distant Honk

Holly Schofield

The **footprints were as bi**g as my snowshoe, the narrow heel a crisp outline, the impression not more than a couple of hours old.

The tracks beelined from the forest edge right through my campsite, growing more erratic as they disappeared on the far side between dark spruce trees hunched under winter burdens. I shuddered, picturing the clown stumbling through last night's snowy darkness: hands flapping in the cold, grinning fiercely, a low hoot escaping from winter-roughened lips. With my heavy down sleeping bag pulled over my head, I hadn't heard a sound, relying on the campfire to keep away predators.

I plodded over to where the tracks entered the clearing, slush sticking to my snowshoes. The sun had risen above the mountaintops, warm for February, warmer than all previous weather records.

A clump of coarse orange hair clung to a hemlock twig, sodden with mud. The email from the game warden had been accurate – the clowns *had* left hibernation early, the earliest yet, the unusually high temperatures triggering abnormal metabolic changes.

The troupe's cave would be much farther up the mountain. I pictured melting ice dripping off the cave ceiling, streaking their greasepaint as they lay curled around one another like rats in a nest. With blank expressions and creaking joints, they'd unfold themselves, straighten their faded blouses on their too-lean frames, and honk softly. Then, they'd burst forth from the cave, one after another after another after another after another, bewildered by the bright sunshine, wanting to sate their terrible hunger.

What could one biologist do? I'd soon finish my dissertation on the wild clowns' shrinking range but there could be no future in coulrology. Since my study had begun, frown lines had etched an oval around my mouth.

At my campsite, I methodically stuffed a daypack for the trip up the mountains. The rest of the gear and food went into my larger backpack. I hefted it, looking for a suitable branch to suspend it from, to keep it safe until I returned. A small bag tumbled out, yellow kernels gleaming beneath plastic packaging. My reserve food, my comfort food. I picked the bag up slowly.

I laid the last of the logs on the remnants of yesterday's fire, although I'd return tired and cold tonight, and fed in scraps of wood until flames fingered up. The last of the butter coated the cooking pot and softened the clinking sound the kernels made as they bounced. A puff of acrid smoke crept out from beneath the lid and I shook the pan harder. I should have waited for coals but, then, patience is not one of humankind's virtues.

Walking in snowshoes takes practice and constant attention to detail. I managed to drink from my water bottle without stopping, juggling the container from hand to hand as I brushed aside wet branches and forged on upwards, inserting my feet into the softening footprints.

My dissertation advisor was convinced that wild clowns would be extinct by 2030. She wanted me to change to cockroach studies and offered to line up space station projects. Her voice rang in my head, drowning out the muttering birds and creaking branches.

You can't base a career on a dying species. Don't back a loser. *Get out while you can.*

I grew warm, opening the ear flaps on my fur-lined hat, letting the breeze flip them up.

As I hiked, hemlock gave way to spruce, which then shrank in stature but not in age. Did a hundred-year-old tree have more wisdom than a sapling? I hoped so. I hoped humankind was gaining more than bare knowledge as it slaughtered thousands of species and chased thousands of others into unsuitable environments.

Wild clowns had their own niche in the ecosystem and every right to perform as nature intended. Every right to hibernate, arise, and eat their fill. Suddenly chilled, I drew my ear flaps close again.

The increasingly slushy tracks zigzagged through the undergrowth, always uphill. Sometimes a slip of the foot made my snowshoes clang together like a bell. Once, a rabbit dashed in front of me, and I windmilled my arms, barely keeping my balance on the steep slope.

The hike gave me a chance to think, to ruminate on the crazy swirling globe we call home. I watched clouds skidding across the sky and pictured the world's animals and people as if we were all under one gigantic blue canvas roof. It didn't matter if climate change was man-made or not, clowns would soon parade out of the tent behind woolly mammoths and dodo birds. My future children would only ever see clowns in captivity.

I threw a snowball straight up and caught it. At this moment, caught in time until the terrain levelled, I could pretend it wasn't so.

The afternoon wind slapped my face as I entered the high meadow. Tracks of varying size and depth criss-crossed the snowy expanse. A curving, wide-mouthed cave entrance slashed through the rock face beyond. Drying sweat made me shiver.

A raven honked. I jumped and then made myself turn a deliberate circle, my overlapping tracks creating a daisy pattern in the snow. No wide white teeth gleamed, no broad half-moon eyes stared at me from the dim forest. The troupe should be far away, hunting until dawn.

The wind increased. I took a quick population estimate from the tracks, not even measuring out a plot, anxious to get back before dark.

That distinctive smell – a mixture of musk, decaying rubber, and decomposing sawdust – billowed out of the low cave. At the dirt-littered entrance, I awkwardly knelt in my bulky parka and snowshoes, then hesitated. I could stick my head in. But why take the risk? The clowns would need me in one piece if I was to be their spokesperson.

From far up the mountain, a distant hoot sounded, low and long, silencing the chatter of the birds.

I pulled the filled baggie from my daypack and gently shook it out on a rock by the entrance. As I headed back downhill, I glanced back at the mound of popcorn – unsure if it was a placation, a gift, or an admission of guilt.

The Day it All Ended

Charlie Jane Anders

Bruce Grinnord parked aslant in his usual spot and ran inside the DiZi Corp. headquarters. Bruce didn't check in with his team or even pause to glare at the beautiful young people having their toes stretched by robots while they sipped macrobiotic goji-berry shakes and tried to imagine ways to make the next generation of gadgets cooler-looking and less useful. Instead, he sprinted for the executive suite. He took the stairs two or three at a time, until he was so breathless he feared he'd have a heart attack before he even finished throwing his career away.

DiZi's founder, Jethro Gruber – Barrons' Young Visionary of the Year five years running – had his office atop the central spire of the funhouse castle of DiZi's offices, in a round glass turret looking down on the employee oxygen bar and the dozen gourmet cafeterias. If you didn't have the key to the private elevator, the only way up was this spiral staircase, which climbed past a dozen Executive Playspaces, and any one of those people could cockblock you before you got to Jethro's pad. But nobody seemed to notice Bruce charging up the stairs, fury twisting his round face, even when he nearly put his foot between the steps and fell into the Moroccan Spice Café.

Bruce wanted to storm into Jethro's office and shout his resignation in Jethro's trendy schoolmaster glasses. He wanted to enter the room already denouncing the waste, the stupidity of it all – but when he reached the top of the staircase, he was so out of breath, he could only wheeze, his guts wrung and cramped. He'd only been in Jethro's office once before: an elegant goldfish bowl with one desk that changed shape (thanks to modular pieces that came out of the floor), a few chairs, and one dot of maroon rug at its center. Bruce stood there, massaging his dumb stomach and taking in the oppressive simplicity.

So Jethro spoke first, the creamy purr Bruce knew from a million company videos. "Hi, Bruce. You're late."

"You're late," Jethro said. "You were supposed to have your crisis of conscience three months ago." He pulled out his Robo-Bop and displayed a personal calendar, which included one entry: "Bruce Has a Crisis of Conscience." It was dated a few months earlier. "What kept you, man?"

It started when Bruce took a wrong turn on the way to work. Actually, he drove to the wrong office – the driving equivalent of a Freudian slip.

He was on the interstate at 7:30, listening to a banjo solo that he hadn't yet learned to play. Out his right window, every suburban courtyard had its own giant ThunderNet tower, just like the silver statue in Bruce's own cul-de-sac – the sleek concave lines and jetstreamed base like a 1950s Googie space fantasy. To his left, almost every passing car had a Car-Dingo bolted to its hood, with its trademark sloping fins and whirling lights. And half the drivers were listening to music, or making Intimate Confessions on their Robo-Bops. Once on the freeway, Bruce could see much larger versions of the ThunderNet tower dotting the landscape, from shopping-mall roofs to empty fields. Plus everywhere he saw giant billboards for DiZi's newest product, the Crado – empty-faced, multicultural babies splayed out in a milk-white, egg-shaped chair that monitored the baby's air supply and temperature in some way that Bruce still couldn't explain.

Bruce was a VP of marketing at DiZi – shouldn't he be able to find something good to say about even one of the company's products?

So this one morning, Bruce got off the freeway a few exits too soon. Instead of driving to the DiZi offices, he went down a feeder road to a dingy strip mall that had offices instead of dry cleaners. This was the route Bruce had taken for years before he joined DiZi, and he felt as though he'd taken the wrong commute by mistake.

Bruce's old parking spot was open, and he could almost pretend time had rolled back, except that he'd lost some hair and gained some weight. He found himself pushing past the white balsawood-and-metal door with the cheap sign saying Eco Gnomic and into the offices, and then he stopped. A roomful of total strangers perched on beanbags and folding chairs turned and stared, and Bruce had no explanation for who he was or why he was there. "Uh," Bruce said.

The Eco Gnomic offices looked like crap compared with DiZi's majesty, but also compared with the last time he'd seen them. Take the giant Intervention Board that covered the main wall: When Bruce had worked there, it'd been covered with millions of multicolored tacks, attached to scraps of incidents. This company is planning a major polluting project, so we mobilize culture-jammer flashmobs here and organize protesters at the public hearing there, like a giant multidimensional chess game covering one wall, deploying patience and playfulness against the massive corporate engine. Now, though, the Intervention Board contained nothing but bad ne280ws, without much in the way of strategies. Arctic Shelf disintegrating, floods, superstorms, droughts, the Gulf Stream stuttering, extinctions like dominoes falling. The office furniture teetered on broken legs, and the same computers from five years ago whined and stammered. The young woman nearest Bruce couldn't even afford a proper Mohawk – her hair grew back in patches on the sides of her head, and the stripe on top was wilting. None of these people seemed energized about saving the planet.

Bruce was about to flee when his old boss, Gerry Donkins, showed up and said, "Bruce! Welcome back to the nonprofit sector, man." Bruce and Gerry wound up spending an hour sitting on crates, drinking expired YooHoo. "Yeah, Eco Gnomic is dying," said Gerry, giant mustache twirling, "but so is the planet."

"I feel like I made a terrible mistake," Bruce said. He looked at the board and couldn't see any pattern to the arrangement of ill omens.

"You did," Gerry replied. "But it doesn't make any difference, and you've been happy. You've been happy, right? We all thought you were happy. How is Marie, by the way?"

"Marie left me two years ago," Bruce said.

"But on the plus side, I've been taking up the banjo."

"Anyway, no offense, but you wouldn't have made a difference if you'd stayed with us. We probably passed the point of no return a while back."

Point of no return. It sounded sexual, or like letting go of a trapeze at the apex of its arc.

"You did the smart thing," said Gerry, "going to work for the flashiest consumer products company and enjoying the last little bit of the ride."

Bruce got back in his Prius and drove the rest of the way to work, past the rows of ThunderNet towers and the smoke from far-off forest fires. This felt like the last day of the human race, even though it was just another day on the steep slope. As Bruce reached the lavender glass citadel of DiZi's offices, he started to go numb inside, like always. But instead, this time, a fury took him, and that's when he charged inside and up the stairs to Jethro's office, ready to shove his resignation down the CEO's throat.

"What do you mean?" Bruce said to Jethro, as his breath came back. "You were *expecting* me to come in here and resign?"

"Something like that." Jethro gestured for Bruce to sit in one of the plain white, absurdly comfortable teacup chairs. He sat cross-legged in the other one, like a yogi in his wide-sleeved linen shirt and camper pants. In person, he looked slightly chubbier and less classically handsome than all his iconic images, but the perfect hipster bowl haircut and sideburns, and those famous glasses, were instantly recognizable. "But like I said: late. The point is, you got here in the end."

"You didn't *engineer* this. I'm not one of your gadgets. This is real. I really am fed up with making pointless toys when the world is about to choke on our filth. I'm done."

"It wouldn't be worth anything if it wasn't real, bro." Jethro gave Bruce one of his conspiratorial/mischievous smiles that made Bruce want to smile back in spite of his soul-deep anger. "That's why we hired you in the first place. You're the canary in the coal mine. Here, look at the org chart."

Jethro made some hand motions, and one glass surface became a screen, which projected an org chart with a thousand names and job descriptions. And there, halfway down on the left, was Bruce's name, with "CANARY IN THE COAL MINE." And a picture of Bruce's head on a cartoon bird's body.

"I thought my job title was junior executive VP for product management," Bruce said, staring at his openmouthed face and those unfurled wings.

Jethro shrugged. "Well, you just resigned, right? So you don't have a title anymore." He made another gesture, and a bright-eyed young thing wheeled a minibar out of the elevator and offered Bruce beer, whiskey, hot sake, coffee, and Mexican Coke. Bruce felt rebellious, choosing a single-malt whiskey, until he realized he was doing what Jethro wanted. He took a swig that burned his throat and eyes.

"So you're quitting; you should go ahead and tell me what you think of my company." Jethro spread his hands and smiled.

"Well." Bruce drank more whiskey and then sputtered. "If you really want to know ... your products are pure evil. You build these sleek little pieces of shit that are designed with all this excess capacity and redundant systems. Have you ever looked at the schematics of the ThunderNet towers? It's like you were *trying* to build something overly complex. And it's the ultimate glorification of form over function – you've been able to convince everybody with disposable income to buy your crap, because people love anything that's ostentatiously pointless. I've had a Robo-Bop for years, and I still don't understand what half the widgets and menu options are for. I don't think anybody does. You use glamour and marketing to convince people they need to fill their lives with empty crap instead of paying attention to the world and realizing how fragile and beautiful it really is. You're the devil."

The drinks fairy had started gawking halfway through this rant, then she seemed to decide it was against her pay grade to hear this. She retreated into the elevator and vanished around the time Bruce said he didn't understand half the stuff his Robo-Bop did. Bruce had fantasized about telling Jethro off for years, and he enjoyed it so much he had tears in his eyes by the end. Even knowing that Jethro had put this moment on his Robo-Bop calendar couldn't spoil it.

Jethro was nodding, as if Bruce had just about covered the bases. Then he made another esoteric gesture, and the glass wall became a screen again. It displayed a PowerPoint slide:

DIZI CORP. PRODUCT STRATEGY
+ Beautiful Objects That Are Functionally Useless
+ Spare Capacity
+ Redundant Systems
+ Overproliferation of Identical but Superficially
  Different Products
+ Form Over Function
+ Mystifying Options and Confusing User Interface

"You missed one, I think," Jethro said. "The one about overproliferation. That's where we convince people to buy three different products that are almost exactly the same, but not quite."

"Wow." Bruce looked at the slide, which had gold stars on it. "You really are completely evil."

"That's what it looks like, huh?" Jethro actually laughed, as he tapped on his Robo-Bop. "Tell you what. We're having a strategy meeting at 3, and we need our canary there. Come and tell the whole team what you told me."

"What's the point?" Bruce felt whatever the next level below despair was. Everything was a joke, *and* he'd been deprived of the satisfaction of being the one to unveil the truth.

"Just show up, man. I promise it'll be entertaining, if nothing else. What else are you going to do with the rest of your day, drive out to the beach and watch the seagulls dying?"

That was exactly what Bruce had planned to do after leaving DiZi. He shrugged. "Sure. I guess I'll go get my toes stretched for a while."

"You do that, Bruce. See you at 3."

The drinks fairy must have gossiped about Bruce, because people were looking at him when he walked down to the main promenade. If there'd been a food court in *2001: A Space Odyssey,* it would have looked like DiZi's employee promenade. Bruce didn't have his toes stretched. Instead, he ate two organic calzones to settle his stomach after the morning whiskey. The calzones made Bruce more nauseated. The people on Bruce's marketing team waved at him in the cafeteria but didn't approach the radioactive man.

Bruce was five minutes early for the strategy meeting, but he was still the last one to arrive, and everyone was staring at him. Bruce had never visited the Executive Meditation Hole, which also doubled as Jethro's private movie theater. It was a big bunker under the DiZi main building with wall carpets and aromatherapy.

"Hey, Bruce." Jethro was lotus-positioning on the dais at the front, where the movie screen would be. "Everybody, Bruce had a Crisis of Conscience today. Big props for Bruce, everybody."

Everyone clapped. Bruce's stomach started turning again, so he put his face in front of one of the aromatherapy nozzles and huffed calming scents. "So Bruce has convinced me that it's time for us to change our product strategy to focus on saving the planet."

"You what?" Bruce pulled away from the soothing jasmine puff. "Are you completely delusional? Have you been surrounded by yes-men and media sycophants for so long that you've lost all sense of reality? It's way, way too late to save the planet, man." Everybody stared at Bruce, until Jethro clapped again. Then everyone else clapped too.

"Bruce brings up a good point," Jethro said. "The timetable is daunting, and we're late. Partly because your Crisis of Conscience was months behind schedule, I feel constrained to point out. In any case, how would we go about meeting this audacious goal? "Enterprise audacity" being one of our corporate buzzsaws, of course. And for that, I'm going to turn it over to Zoe. Zoe?"

Jethro went and sat in the front row, and a big screen appeared up front. A skinny woman in a charcoal-gray suit got up and used her Robo-Bop to control a presentation.

"Thanks, Jethro," the stick-figure woman, Zoe, said. She had perfect Amanda Seyfried hair. "It really comes down to what we call product versatility." She clicked on a picture of a nice midrange car with a swooshy device bolted to its roof. "Take the Car-Dingo, for example.

Various people raised their hands and offered slogans like "It makes a Prius feel like a muscle car," or "It awesomeizes your ride."

"Exactly!" Zoe smiled. She clicked the next slide over, and proprietary specs for the Car-Dingo came up. They were so proprietary, Bruce had never seen them. Bruce struggled to make sense of all those extra connections and loops, going right into the engine. She pulled up similar specs for the ThunderNet tower, full of secret logic. Another screen showed all those nonsensical Robo-Bop menus, suddenly unlocking and making sense.

"Wait a minute." Bruce was the only one standing up, besides Zoe. "So you're saying all these devices were dual-function all this time? And in all the hundreds of hellish product meetings I've sat through, you never once mentioned this fact?"

"Bruce," Jethro said from the front row, "we've got a little thing at DiZi called the Culture of Listening. That means no interrupting the presentation until it's finished, or no artisanal cookies for you."

Bruce sighed and climbed over someone to find a seat and listened to another hour of corporate "buzzsaws." At one point he could have sworn Zoe said something about "end-user velocitization." One thing Bruce did understand, in the gathering haze: Even though DiZi officially frowned on the cheap knockoffs of its products littering the Third World, the company had gone to great lengths to make sure those illicit copies used the exact same specs as the real items.

Just as Bruce was passing out from boredom, Jethro thanked Zoe and said, "Now let's give Bruce the floor. Bruce, come on down." Bruce had to thump his own legs to wake them up, and when he reached the front, he'd forgotten all the things he was dying to say an hour earlier. The top echelons of DiZi management stared, waiting for him to say something.

"Uh." Bruce's head hurt. "What do you want me to say?"

Jethro stood up next to Bruce and put an arm around him. "This is where your Crisis of Conscience comes in, Bruce dude. Let's just say, as a thought embellishment, that we could fix it." ("Thought embellishment" was one of Jethro's buzzsaws.)

Jethro handed Bruce a Robo-Bop with a pulsing Yes/No screen. "It's all on you, buddy. You push Yes, we can make a difference here. There'll be some disruptions, people might be a mite inconvenienced, but we can ameliorate some of the problems. Push No, and things go on as they are. But bear in mind – if you push Yes, you're the one who has to explain to the people."

Bruce still didn't understand what he was saying yes to, but he hardly cared. He jabbed the Yes button with his right thumb. Jethro whooped and led him to the executive elevator, so they could watch the fun from the roof.

"It should be almost instantaneous," Jethro said over his shoulder as he hustled into the lift. "Thanks to our patented "snaggletooth" technology that makes all our products talk to each other. It'll travel around the world like a wave. It's part of our enterprise philosophy of Why-Not-Now."

The elevator lurched upward, and in moments they had reached the roof. "It's starting," Jethro said. He pointed to the nearest ThunderNet tower. The sleek lid was opening up like petals, until the top resembled a solar dish. And a strange haze was gathering over the top of it.

"This technology has been around for years, but everybody said it was too expensive to deploy on a widespread basis," Jethro said with a wink. "In a nutshell, the tops of the towers contain a photocatalyst material, which turns the CO2 and water in the atmosphere into methane and oxygen. The methane gets stored and used as an extra power source. The tower is also spraying an amine solution into the air that captures more CO2 via a proprietary chemical reaction. That's why the ThunderNets had to be so pricey."

Just then, Bruce felt a vibration from his own Robo-Bop. He looked down and was startled to see a detailed audit of Bruce's personal carbon footprint – including everything he'd done to waste energy in the past five years.

"And hey, look at the parking lot," Jethro said. All the Car-Dingos were reconfiguring themselves, snaking new connections into the car engines. "We're getting most of those vehicles as close to zero emissions as possible, using amines that capture the cars' CO2. You can use the waste heat from the engine to regenerate the amines." But the real gain would come from the cars' GPSs, which would start nudging people to carpool whenever another Car-Dingo user was going to the same destination, using a "packet-switching" model to optimize everyone's commute for greenness. Refuse to carpool, and your car might start developing engine trouble – and the Car-Dingos, Bruce knew, were almost impossible to remove.

As for the Crados? Jethro explained how they were already hacking into every appliance in people's homes, to make them energy-efficient whether people wanted them to be or not.

Zoe was standing at Bruce's elbow. "It's too late to stop the trend, or even reverse all the effects," she said over the din of the ThunderNet towers. "But we can slow it drastically, and our most optimistic projections show major improvements in the medium term."

"So all this time – all this hellish time – you had the means to make a difference, and you just ... sat on it?" Bruce said. "What the fuck were you thinking?"

"We wanted to wait until we had full product penetration." Jethro had to raise his voice now; the ThunderNet towers were actually thundering for the first time ever. "And we needed people to be ready. If we had just come out and told the truth about what our products actually did, people would rather die than buy them. Even after Manhattan and Florida. We couldn't give them away. But if we claimed to be making overpriced, wasteful pieces of crap that destroy the environment? Then everybody would need to own two of them."

"So my Crisis of Conscience—" Bruce could only finish that sentence by wheeling his arms.

"We figured the day when you no longer gave a shit about your own future would be the day when people might accept this," Jethro said, patting Bruce on the back like a father, even though he was younger.

"Well, thanks for the mind games." Bruce had to shout now. "I'm going to go explore something I call my culture of drunkenness."

"You can't leave, Bruce," Jethro yelled in his ear. "This is going to be a major disruption, everyone's gadgets going nuts at once. There will be violence and wholesale destruction of public property. There will be chain saw rampages. There may even be Twitter snark. We need you to be out in front on this, explaining it to the people."

Bruce looked out at the dusk, red-and-black clouds churning as millions of ThunderNet towers blasted them with scrubber beams. Even over that racket, the chorus of car horns and shouts as people's Car-Dingos suddenly had minds of their own started to ring from the highway. Bruce turned and looked into the gleam of his boss's schoolmaster specs. "Fuck you, man," he said. Followed a moment later by "I'll do it."

"We knew we could count on you." Jethro turned to the half-dozen or so executives cluttering the roof deck behind him. "Big hand for Bruce, everybody." Bruce waited until they were done clapping, then leaned over the railing and puked his guts out.

Charlie Jane Anders is the author of *All the Birds in the Sky* and the forthcoming *The City in the Middle of the Night*. She used to be an editor with *io9*, a site about science, science fiction, fantasy and futurism, and she still organizes a monthly reading series called *Writers With Drinks*.

Illustrated by Sydney Jordan

Classic time travel stories from the last four decades gathered together in print for the very first time in this special edition

Published by Shoreline of Infinity Publications

paperback £10

also in ebook formats

available in all good bookshops or from

www.shorelineofinfinity.com

The Namesake

Truth is Freedom

by adam e bradbury

She is a namesake of the Family Trevelian.

She works the land and praises the Living Saints with all her heart.

When faith turns to violence her world is torn apart.

She must survive.

Our world depends on her.

Available on Amazon

THE GALACTIC FESTIVAL

by

Paul Holmes

Shoreline of Infinity's master puzzler

New puzzles to take your brain to a higher level

Available from

www.shorelineofinfinity.com

and all good bookshops

£8.50 paperback

£3.50 for ebook (PDF)

Last of the Guerilla Gardeners

David L Clements

They came for Percy Thrower last night. I was on my way to deliver some *Afghan Purple* seeds when I saw the first police car. I turned the corner and saw a fleet of them parked outside her house, complete with sniffer dogs and a space-suited forensic team heading for her potting shed.

I averted my eyes and walked past on the opposite side of the road, feeling the packet of illegal seeds in my back pack broadcasting my guilt. As I left her road the sterilization van arrived, its flame throwers ready to destroy Percy's irreplaceable collection of plants.

I got away. The others weren't so lucky. As I waited for the bus I checked our secure server and realized they were rolling up the whole network. Monty had been the first, but in catapulting a package of herb seeds into Buckingham Palace gardens he'd gone too far. But his arrest had been the trigger for raids across the country. Bob had sent out a warning as they smashed down his door, but they'd been ready for us all. If I hadn't been on a delivery run they would have caught me as well.

I couldn't go home, and most of the people I trust had already been picked up. I stayed on the bus as it passed my stop and headed into central London. The clean up crews were all too obvious, torching collections of wild flowers in the roadside beds I'd seeded from bus windows while commuting.

All the hard work, all the beautiful, irreplaceable diversity, stamped out by commercial greed. If I'd had the machinery with me I'd've lept off the bus and seeded the Palace gardens myself.

Percy had started the whole thing with a few prophetic words: "Biology is the biggest peer-to-peer copying system on the planet. Now they've eliminated file sharing they'll come for the seed sharers."

She'd been a university botanist for years but left academia for horticulture when it became clear that all the grants were controlled by big agribusiness. We knew we were in trouble when Kew was sold off and Henry Doubleday broken up. Their vast seed collections became the intellectual property of a few huge corporations. Unlisenced seeds were already illegal to sell, but now the companies owned all the rare strains collectors had been sharing freely for decades. Percy saw what would happen - they'd want to control it all.

At first we tried to stop them. There were protests, lobbies, and mass marches. *Gardeners' Question Time* became such a political hot potato it was cancelled by the BBC. And then came the Chelsea Flower Show riots.

We were called economic terrorists, threatening profits from high cost, high yield, terminator-gene-strains that would both feed the world and soak up excess CO_2. But we just wanted tasty vegetables from our own gardens, unusual flowers smelling as good as they looked, and the opportunity to eat the occasional purple carrot. Nobody cared until the first self propagating, superplants were found growing beside a road in Norfolk.

"Businessmen don't understand that biology is a lot messier than digital copying," said Percy as we discussed the development in her potting shed. "I can think of a dozen perfectly natural ways the terminator gene might have failed. A single cosmic ray taking out the right base pair would be enough!" But scientific good sense was never going to stand up to irate politicians demanding that something must be done. Fines became prison sentences, special seed squads were established, and we were forced underground. Home gardens were no longer safe, so we became guerilla gardeners - a secret society sharing seeds and planting contraband crops in public spaces, tending them at night or just scattering seed far and wide to let nature take its course. That's when the network started and we adopted our *noms de vert*.

We were too successful. Nature was indeed the great copier. Our wilder strains could fend for themselves and started to spread. The gloves finally came off when the director of Smaxo's agricultural division found a clump of illegal Pink Brandywine tomatoes growing at the bottom of his garden and carpeted the Prime Minister. Of course Monty and his catapult didn't help.

Now the only guerilla gardner left is me. I've collected my stash from a station locker along with Monty's seed catapult. The sleeper train to Fort William goes through a lot of isolated country. The clean up crews won't cover all this ground in one season, so some of my seeds are going out of the window.

As for the rest ... There are still islands off the Scottish coast contaminated by bioweapon testing in World War Two. People aren't allowed there and there are no sheep or rabbits, but their climate is mild. The catapult has enough range to reach the shore from a rented or stolen boat. Or I could go ashore and make sure the seeds are properly planted. They will do well on the islands, even if I don't. In a few years the islands will become a reserve for natural, non-commercial diversity no matter what happens to me, the last guerilla gardener.

David L Clements is a professional astrophysicist working at Imperial College London on extragalactic astronomy and observational cosmology.
He has had stories published in *Analog, Nature, Clarkesworld, Shoreline of Infinity* and numerous anthologies. His first short story collection, *Disturbed Universes*, was published in 2016.
Twitter: @davecl42 Blog: davecl.wordpress.com

The Last Days of the Lotus Eaters

Leigh Harlen

The earth, and the creatures in it ate her flesh, but the tree kept her bones, its roots wrapped around and entwined every remaining bit of her. Wind stirred the branches of the tree and it tickled as if it were her own leaves being caressed and tossed about. Birds perched on the branches and she felt their hopping feet and heard the chirps of their offspring. She remembered what it was to have a beating heart, breath in her lungs, and feel the wind toss her hair about, so that it tickled her face. She was awake, but not alive.

Lita wasn't forgotten immediately. After she was buried, when she was only half awake, the roots not yet able to reach her bones, she heard her parents weep above her. Every day they came to wail and lament and she hated them. Hated them for not believing her. When her flesh was consumed and the roots fused to her bones huge blossoms appeared on the tree that for years had produced fewer and more pitiful flowers as it died little by little. Now they were rich and fragrant, dense and beautiful in a way she had heard the old folks talk about when they were melancholy and nostalgic and flushed with too much wine.

Her parents gasped, taking the blossoming to be a sign, a comfort. She felt the tug as they each plucked one, the grinding of their teeth as they chewed, reveling in its sweetness. The flowers slid down their throats, into their acid filled bellies and then plucked out their memories, their fear, and their grief. It all passed into her, tasting like bitter dust. Her mother's agony as she was birthed, and her father's joy mixed with terror as he held her tiny body in his arms for the first time, thinking how fragile she was and how much his life was about to change. She saw herself running through the woods and understood the fear they had shoved down brought on by her careless certainty that no matter where she ran or how high she jumped she would never be hurt. And she felt the doubt that had crept in when she told them over and over that the sky shouldn't be so black, so empty, and there should be life beyond the walls of their little village. Their minds were emptied of all that made them doubtful and unhappy while she felt swollen and sick.

At night, the wind stirred the blossoms and carried pollen through the air and into the lungs of the sleeping villagers, dulling the fears that had been growing as the tree died. When people heard that it was producing flowers again, they came to eat them and one by one their fears and doubts were erased completely and buried in her.

Only the priests took vows not to eat the flowers, though they were also soothed by its pollen, their faith fortified and guilt dulled if not erased. They read secret texts that told them what to do to keep the tree from dying and they needed to remember. All except one, one priest was given leave to break his vows and eat the blossoms. The one who had killed her.

He walked up to the tree and picked a flower. With his other hand he took out a flask and raised it to the tree. "I truly am sorry, Lita, you were a remarkable young woman. But you were wrong." He took a sip of wine and ate the flower and gave her his memories.

The night he heard that there was a little girl who talked about stars and the end of the universe, he was relieved and terrified. The tree was dying and they needed to revive it, but he had hoped that necessity would come when he had passed his position on to a younger priest. He stayed awake all night, reading the holy book to fortify his nerves and staring into the flickering light of a candle knowing it would still be years before the ritual could be performed, the text and his conscience demanded certainty.

In the bright morning she was running through the grass, running so fast she felt like maybe she could outrun the end of the world. She stopped when he stood in front of her.

"Lita, could I walk with you for a little while?" he said.

She had been taught to trust and respect the priests and though she wanted to keep running, she nodded.

"I heard you telling stories at the market yesterday," he said.

"They aren't stories. The night sky is empty and it didn't used to be. I read about stars in the library, there were so many of them and they were so beautiful that people wrote poetry about them and used them to navigate. There was a moon and there were huge oceans. Entire planets where people lived and travelled. Not just one little village with an empty sky," she said.

He smiled. "Most people would say those are just stories, fairy tales. It's unusual for a girl your age to believe such things."

She glared at him. "They aren't made up. Why would so many of the ancient writers all make-up something like that?" She wouldn't be reasoned with, not about this. She had told her parents, her grandparents, her friends and their parents since she was old enough to look at the sky and wonder why there was nothing but the sun in all that big black emptiness. No one believed her, she had hoped the priest would be different, that he would know some arcane secrets and share them with her.

Having consumed those secrets, she understood he was different, he did know. He had wanted her to say, "Yes, you're right. They're just stories." He wanted her to take it all back because he liked her, he liked that she was smart and not afraid to argue with him. He didn't want to have to kill her, but there was also a coldness in him, a small shard at the center that made him certain that he could, that gave him a feeling of righteousness. He was doing what was best for everyone. What was one little girl's life in the face of chaos and despair for an entire people?

He left her alone with her confusion but he didn't leave her completely. She often saw him out of the corner of her eye, listening to her conversations just a little too intently, watching her when the villagers gathered to dine together with a dark and contemplative expression.

A couple of years after that first strange conversation, he stopped her while she was walking home from school.

"Would it be alright if I walked with you?" he said.

"Of course." Even if he was a bit strange, her parents would send her to bed without dinner if she was rude to a priest.

"Tell me, do you still think the sky is too empty?" he said.

"I know it is."

"What if you're right? What would be the purpose of knowing?"

Lita hadn't thought about that. She'd spent her life so angry and frustrated that no one believed her that she hadn't thought much about why she wanted so badly for them to know beyond simple vindication.

"The sun is a star. Whatever happened to the stars could happen to our sun too and we'd all die."

"And what would you do about it?"

"I-I don't know. I just think people should know."

"Would it make them happier to know if there's nothing to be done about it? What would be the point of being good, of having children, working for a future that might be snuffed out with the sun at any moment?" he said.

She frowned. "Why would knowing the truth mean people don't do those things?"

"Does that belief make you happier? Because it seems to me you don't have any interest in those things. You don't have many friends and you've never expressed interest in having a boyfriend or a girlfriend like other girls your age. Your teachers say you've never talked about wanting to be a farmer, a builder, a healer, a baker, or any other role in the village when you finish your studies. Do you see yourself having a future?"

She wasn't unhappy, but it was true that she took little interest in planning for the future and her insistence that the world had ended and they were the last to know drove people away and gave her a reputation for being strange.

"I don't object to doing those things, they just don't seem very important," she said.

"I think you are quite remarkable in that. Most people who believed that would lose all hope, they would do nothing but wallow in their despair and possibly act out in rage and be violent to others or themselves. But even if everyone took the knowledge as well as you but the sun was still there and shining bright for fifty years, a hundred years, we would still need to plan for a future. We would still need food and people to heal us when we're sick or hurt. We would still be better for having lived full lives."

"Are you trying to tell me that I should stop telling the truth?"

"I am asking you to consider that maybe other people should not know it."

"But they're believing a lie, it's not right. I don't know how to explain why it's not right, but it's not."

The priest sighed. She understood now that he was seeking some kind of acceptance or consent from her to do what he knew must be done to sooth his own conscience. But at the time she had been confused, he was talking to her as if he might believe her but it gave her no peace because he was raising questions she didn't have answers to and making her feel foolish. It was evident to her that it was true and people should know it for the very simple reason that it was wrong not to know the truth.

The priest came to her one more time shortly before she was to finish her schooling. She was sitting in the grass reading from a dusty book she had found in the library, a book about cosmology and theories about the creation of the universe. It had been filed as science fiction and forgotten by everyone but her.

"I hear you've decided to become a teacher, Lita," he said.

She nodded. Although the priest made her uncomfortable, she was also happy to see him. In her sixteen years, he was the only person who had ever engaged with her about her belief that the universe was ending, even though she left each conversation feeling confused and chastised, it was a relief to be taken seriously and she felt more prepared to argue with him each time.

"Would you care to walk with me a bit?" he said.

She closed her book and slipped it into her bag. "Okay."

"What led you to want to teach?"

"There are so many things we've forgotten. Technology that could make our lives easier and maybe even save us if someone with a brain that works just the right way learns about it."

"You still think the world is ending?"

"I know the universe is ending. Everything is being pulled further and further apart and soon it's going to start getting too cold to grow things, then it will get too cold to live on the surface and we'll need to go underground, and eventually it will be too cold to live anywhere. We need to prepare."

"That doesn't sound like something anyone could prepare for. If annihilation is inevitable, why not let people live happily until the end?" he said.

"Maybe it is inevitable. But we would last longer and we might have a chance to avoid it for a long time if only people knew. And I think that's worth the fear and even the despair."

They came to the dying tree and he stopped and looked at her. "You are very certain of yourself."

She was proud, for the first time she felt she came out of a conversation with the priest as the victor. "I am."

He pulled a small flask from his jacket. "I still disagree. I think you are young and idealistic and want to believe that people think and act like you, that they would accept inevitable doom with grace and resilience. But I do admire you."

"Thank you," she said.

He raised the flask. "To the moral certainty of youth and to the intellect and tenacity you have grown into so well." He took a drink – although she now knew that he let it graze his lips and slosh back inside.

He passed the flask to her. "Just a sip, I can't have it said a holy man is getting young women drunk."

She hesitated, but she was flattered and her parents only let her have wine

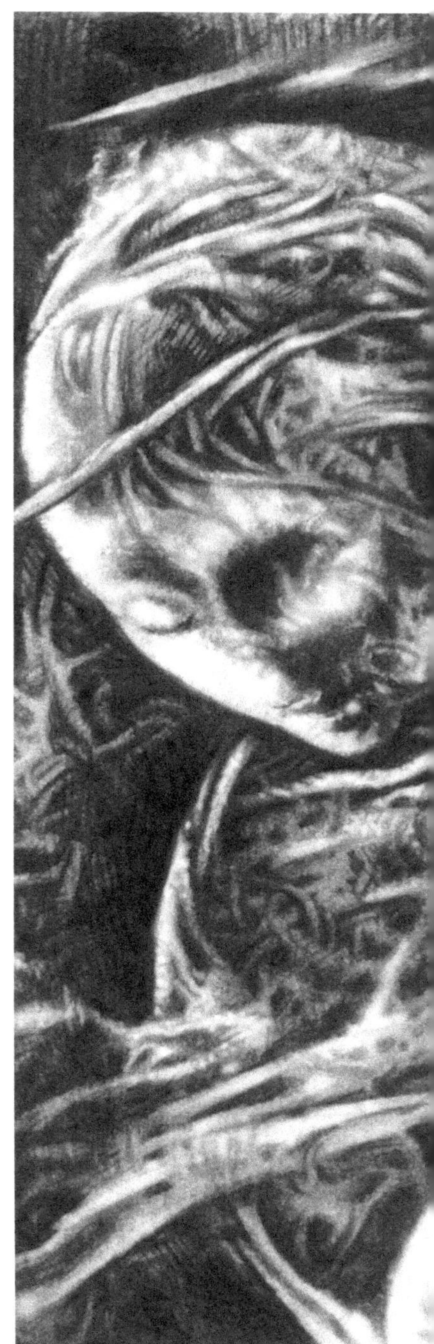

on holy days. She took a sip. It tasted like vinegar and ash and in just seconds she was unconscious.

The priest believed that the drug would prevent her from waking up and feeling any part of the ritual, but he was wrong. The tree did not share the priest's minimal compassion and the ritual was not one that it allowed its sacrifice to sleep through. She also knew from being forced to carry his memories that even if he had known, he would have buried her still alive at the base of the tree anyway, such was his faith and conviction.

When she woke, she choked on the dirt and screamed as the roots bore into her like hungry fingers, ripping into her soft skin, ravenous for the life bleeding out of her body and the taste of the knowledge that had marked her for death. It had been a long time since it had been given a new life to nourish it.

As the blossom pulled out and transferred the priest's memories of her and of how he had liked her and how he had vomited when he heard her muffled screams coming up through the ground, she wanted to tell him that she still knew he was wrong and that she still intended to be a teacher in her own way.

He walked away, his mouth still sweet from the blossom he had consumed and his mind emptied of terrible memories and doubts about the righteousness of his actions. He returned to the priesthood a blank slate, prepared to watch for the next girl who wanted to know why the sky was so dark.

Years passed and her parents and all the people she had known when she was alive died, their names soon as forgotten as her own to the handful who struggled to survive on the increasingly hostile surface. The sun still shone in the sky, but it looked smaller, the plants began dying, and the people above whispered through frostbitten fingers, "Winter is almost over, summer is on its way." But she knew winter would never end and soon the people above forgot that there had been such a thing as summer.

The tree alone stayed green and every night it spread pollen on the wind so that they could believe winter was all there was and they shouldn't look too hard at the sky. As her bones crumbled, the blossoms began to shrink and there were less and less of them each year so the people saved eating them only for holy days and slowly their doubts began to grow.

A young girl came and sat at the base of the tree.

"I don't have any friends. They all think I'm strange. Yesterday a group of big kids tried to throw me in the river because I told them winter didn't used to last forever. It used to get warm and green. I read it in a book. A little kid was swinging on a rope and they jumped into a lake and didn't get sick and have to be warmed up afterwards. They picked flowers, not like from you where we eat them, but just because there were so many and they were pretty. I wish you weren't just a tree so you could talk to me." The girl stood and ran away.

Soon after, the girl's teacher came to eat the blossoms and she swallowed his doubts and the fear he felt when a priest came and asked about her, wanting to know what she wrote about in her school essays and if she had any plans for the future.

The possibility of a future was almost gone. Soon it would be too cold for anyone to survive on the surface and they would need to go underground and start learning the tools to extend their survival as long as possible. And just like she had known, that little girl would be certain that people deserved to know and that immunity to the lie marked her for death because there were no words to convince a zealous and righteous priest that she was right. She couldn't save her own life and she couldn't return the possibility that knowledge gave to the rest of the village, only the tree could do that.

She didn't have much time if any knowledge returned to the village was to be of any help, but she would have to wait until the girl was a little older, old enough to read and understand more than just children's stories.

The new priest came to the girl again. The tree was dying fast and he didn't wait as long between conversations as the old priest had for Lita.

The girl came to sit at the base of the tree as had become her custom.

"I wish I knew how to explain to the priest that it's important for people to know the truth, I felt stupid. It's just so obvious, it doesn't make sense why I'm the only who sees it. You're starting to die, but you're still green and nothing else is, it's not normal, I don't care how 'spiritually important' a tree is, it can't survive the cold so well," the girl said.

Lita felt hope for the first time since she died. She reached out, one of the branches flicked and the backpack she had been carrying the day the priest had buried her slipped from the hole where it had fallen unnoticed.

The girl picked it up and opened it. One by one took the books out and flipped through the pages.

"Did you do that?" She looked amazed and suspicious but she sat at the base of the tree and read for hours. When night descended she put the books back in the bag and ran home.

Even though they did not affect her, the girl stopped eating the blossoms on holy days so Lita had no idea what the girl might have figured out from the books or about who they had belonged to.

One night, under cover of darkness, the girl came out to the tree with a ladder and one by one, plucked off each blossom and burned them in a pile.

There was terror and outrage in the village the next day when they discovered all of the flowers were gone, although no one knew who had done it. It was an ingenious idea, and Lita was delighted by the girl's cleverness, but the blossoms grew back. During the weeks it took however, questions and doubts flourished in the little village.

The girl's parents came to the tree and prayed. They ate two of the small blossoms even though they knew it was forbidden outside holy days to preserve the few remaining. They were deeply troubled by their daughter's insistence that the tree was somehow blinding everyone to the fact that the world was ending, that the sky shouldn't be empty, and the sun used to be nearer. And they were growing distrustful of the priest who came and asked them about her, if she told them her theories and if they thought she believed what she said or if she was just a girl telling stories.

That night, the girl came one more time. She opened a bottle of alcohol and poured it on the tree and set it ablaze.

In the ground, Lita screamed silently, not since the tree had ripped her apart had she felt pain like that. She thrashed and the tree above shook and groaned. People ran from the village and threw buckets of water on it.

It smoldered for days, but the fire did not kill the tree, not completely, she wasn't sure if the tree could be killed. But it was badly hurt and would not be able to grow blossoms for a long time. Desperate for nourishment to heal itself, it gripped her fragile bones in its roots as if it were wringing the last drops of water out of a sponge. It squeezed until her bones turned to dust and the memories and knowledge she had swallowed for so many years soaked the earth. With no other soul to carry that burden, the hungry roots drank in all of the secrets she had kept for so long.

After several months, the tree began to regrow and a few pitiful, tiny flowers bloomed, still fueled by the last bits of Lita's life it had stored in its roots. That night, when the wind blew it carried pollen laced with generations of knowledge and memories, dusting the sleeping survivors with doubt and questions.

The next morning, the girl awoke to a village gripped with chaos and panic. She looked at the tree, blackened and skeletal, looming on the hill over the village and whispered a thank you.

Leigh Harlen's work has been published in magazines and anthologies including *Aurealis, Bards and Sages Quarterly*, and *Dark Moon Digest*. They live in Seattle with their partner and a mischief of rats. When not writing, they're usually found petting strangers' dogs or enthusing about bats.

Follow them on Twitter @leighharlen.

We Have Magnetic Trees

Ian Hunter

H**eading home we came to Little Gasko**, our closest village, straight into a traffic jam caused by a group of 'Free to Be Fatties' demonstrators. Some of them were walking around in their underwear, others wore wobbly fat suits, a couple looked like orange sumo wrestlers.

"Who are these people, Dad?" Mark asked, on one of the rare occasions he looked up. While beside him, Nick's head was still lowered, lost in a game.

"Just a protest group," I told him, frowning as we slowed to join the queue of cars, my mind doing calculations. Take a right, then a left, then another left. Would that bring us out beyond the protestors? I cursed myself for not bringing the satnav but that was in Ali's Car.

Two people were waddling down beside the line of cars. One handed out leaflets, another had a tray of nibbles. I rolled down the window and sniffed. Somewhere up ahead there was a barbeque. I pulled down my sun visor and changed its mode, lens zooming down the main road.

"Shit," I muttered, flipping up the visor. Someone had pointed in our direction, faces were turning towards us. A couple of guys with long hair and faces dotted with piercings started to jog closer as quickly as they could in their fat suits.

I looked in the mirror, signalled and swung across the road just as a hand beat against the roof of the Land Rover.

Ali let her window down an inch. "Hey, we've got children in here!"

"Why are you letting your land be experimented on?" a man with metal hoops round his nostrils asked, breath close enough to mist the window.

"Because the world needs food that can survive our lousy weather!" I shouted back, turning the car round, and having no choice but to mount the pavement. No way was I going to attempt a three-point turn. They'd lie down behind me in protest. Force me to run over one of them and burst their suit before they farted off through the air to land in a tree or the pond in the village square.

The other one pulled at the door handle on my side. "This is just the start!" he yelled. "Crops that can beat the rain can be modified to warp your thinking! Free to be Fatties!" he shouted, again and again, hand slapping the car in time to his chant. "Free to be Fatties! Free to be Fatties! Free to be Fatties!"

"You're not even fat," I snarled at him, feeling hot and angry as we headed out of the village and the start of the maze of country roads we would have to take to get back home.

"I'm really sorry," Ricky said, his image scratchy, shrugging into the webcam as we connected on Skype. "They say the skies won't be safe for weeks."

What could I say? Ricky was employed by WEErd Wonders as project leader, to make sure they harvested the hybrid plant we called the Clingers, the new crop that was being trialled on our land. He wasn't working for me. His dad had been in the wrong place at the wrong time, smashing into a pile-up on the Great Ocean Road, as he headed north from Melbourne on a business trip. I couldn't blame the kid for wanting to leave and fly across the world to check on his father who was in a bit of a state. Broken limbs and tangled innards, to use one of my technical terms. Now Ricky was in the wrong place at the wrong time, stuck in Australia as flights were grounded all because of a volcanic eruption further away from Cairns than my farm back in Scotland.

"Nothing you can do about it, except maybe take a slow boat to China," I eventually replied, half-joking. "Just get back here in time for the first leaves to appear."

We said our goodbyes and the brightness died on the screen. I stared at my own slightly warped reflection, my own ghost curving away from me. The room behind was full of "stuff" as Ali called it, belonging to my father, or my grandfather, all sheep farmers, and I was the last sheep farmer standing, or sitting – or at least I used to be. I reached out and closed the laptop, thinking. Nothing can go wrong, so Ricky had said, but that didn't allow for cars slamming into each other above miles and miles of beautiful beaches on the Great Ocean Road, or passengers stranded by volcanic ash. I turned my head listening to the wind racing around inside the chimney, loosening stones. Sleet was falling outside the window. This was supposed to be Spring, but it isn't these days. Spring is a moveable season that sometimes doesn't happen at all. For WEErd Wonders this project is just one of several, but for me and the family it is everything, our livelihoods, maybe even our futures.

We used to get our sheep stolen. There were organised gangs on quad bikes, sometimes with a van, or a lorry, sometimes bearing crossbows – or a gun if they really meant business. If a drone showed me someone carrying a gun then I didn't try and intervene. Then there was Joe Bloggs out in his car, who looked over a hedge into a field and suddenly decided he would like some lamb. If I was lucky I would get a fence alert, and one of the drones could capture the registration number of the car, and the police would be waiting for them when they got home. More often than not, these people weren't organised criminals, not like the gangs, but still smart enough to clone a number plate when they drove into the countryside, maybe even from the same model of car. Right car, wrong number. Private drones aren't allow to follow any vehicles on to the motorway, for fear they cause an accident. All of that – the organised gangs, the tourist rustlers, as I call them, and the weather – adds up to the fact that we aren't a sheep farm any more. It's too dammed hard. The weather is unpredictable. Seasons come when seasons shouldn't. Incessant downpours, even blizzards near lambing time, burying sheep about to give birth in feet of snow.

So hundreds of years of sheep farming has more or less stopped with me. Insert guilt here. Sure we keep the odd lamb, and the odd calf. The kids look after them. We tried having a farm shop, but couldn't get the range of products and they are too expensive compared to the supermarkets. Times are hard and people can't afford things that are double the price, not in the volumes we would need to sell. We even tried to make our own ice cream for a while, still do, occasionally, but the novelty has worn off. Holiday cottages? You name it, we've tried the lot.

Ricky's boss from WEErd Wonders, Bill Mathers, was standing in the Tech-barn they had built next to some old barns of my own. He was accompanied by some guys in white coats wielding tablets. They were doing some major modifications to the unit the drones passed through on a conveyor belt, which attached and removed the sprays the drones carried. I looked up at the sound of rain drumming on the roof. You would have thought they could have muffled that noise somehow with their fancy portable building, sometimes the sound of rain falling drives me crazy.

"We can do everything remotely from here," Bill explained. "Since there's not much of the trial period left."

I didn't know what to say. "You're not replacing Ricky?"

He shook his head. "It's a monitoring job, and tinkering with the sprays the drones deliver. They can still collect soil and air samples, see what the enemy is up to, so to speak." His sweeping arm, gestured to the rows of equipment and machinery. On one surface three monitors showed graphs and waves and bands of numbers that meant nothing to me. "We can counteract everything they come up with using what's here already."

"Are you sure? Really?"

"Unless they want to scorch your earth, and they'd have to get past the Magnetic Trees to do it." He snorted. "There's enough scorched earth around anyway. Who needs more of it, eh?"

No-one, I thought, looking out of the window to the line of trees WEErd Wonders had planted. Staring as if I could see the land beyond them.

Like Bill said, we have Magnetic Trees. They are not really magnetic, of course, but they are there to shield the farm and our fields, soak up any bad particles that might ruin our test crop. Bad particles that have somehow managed to stray here accidentally, because there is a lot of bad stuff in the air these days, just drifting about. Or it's bad stuff deliberately released by groups who are against the use of nano-technology in food production, although not so much against it, that they won't use their own bugs to get their way. Our adversaries are the 'Free to Be Fatties' who think growing crops to beat the weather will just be the first step in manipulating food supplies. Adding vitamins and minerals to food is good for the consumer, but they fear that things will be added to the crops that switch off parts of your brain, make you feel full, make you eat less, make scarce food resources go a little bit further in an overpopulated world with a crap climate.

Apart from the Magnetic Trees, being involved with WEErd Wonders means we get top of the range drones for spraying and security purposes. Trespassers beware, if they can get past the newly erected fences which border the farm, and you would need to be a pole-vaulter to manage that. We also get a state of the art smart fridge. The *Blue Sapphire* they call it, after Queen

Elizabeth's 65 years on the throne. I admit those thick blue stripes are more than a little garish. Ali hates them and wants me to paint the fridge white. I'm worried that might compromise the magic that works inside the thing so she'll just have to put up with the blue stripes for as long as the fridge works. Given it came with a lifetime guarantee and downloads its own updates, I expect that to be a long, long time.

We were airing one of the holiday cottages when Ali delivered her bombshell. The cottage was cold and smelled damp, but the view was nice, especially this early in the day. Fields stretching to rolling hills, topped with clouds. Some of what I could see belonged to us. You could see which part by the large WEErd Wonders fence marking the boundary.

"Maybe we should sell up," she said, back turned to me.

I could feel myself swallowing as I looked at her. "You think? I mean if this works we won't need to worry about keeping the wolf from the door, just down at the gate, but…"

"Suppose they take their business to other farms?" Ali said, concern etched on her face when she turned round. "Farmers more desperate than us? Who'll take any offer?"

"We could be their main test site," I insisted. "This is just the start, Ali. If the Clingers can beat the weather then you can start tinkering with them. Try and get better yields, add in more vitamins and nutrients."

"So 'Free to be Fatties' are right after all?" she said, eyebrows raised. "It is all about making people thinner?"

"Healthier," I countered. "There's too many people and not enough food for everyone. The planet is gubbed. Too much water in some places and not enough water in others. Guess which part we live in?"

"I know it makes sense," she said, striking another match too hard and snapping it. "This is about trying to grow food that can survive constant downpours, but as you said, it'll soon be about growing food that makes people feel fuller, even when they eat less."

"Is that a bad thing? Look at the smart fridge they gave us. The packaging reacts with the food and keeps it fresher for longer. The fridge reacts with the packaging and makes the food last even longer than that." She shook her head. "Where does it stop, Grant? Food that can make you feel full might become food that can make you feel happy, content?"

"What's wrong with that? Food has always affected people's emotions, their cravings. People get hooked on certain foods, or need some at certain times. Like chocolate or coffee."

"Yeah, because they are addicted to caffeine," the green tea drinker of the family reminded me. "Like I said, we could sell the place, think of the development potential."

"It's Green Belt so you can't build here," I told her bluntly as something childish stirred to life inside me, wanting to shoot down every suggestion she came up with. "Besides the construction boom is long gone. Small, energy efficient units are what's hot, and in the city, not in the countryside."

"Then sell the farm to the company and let them run it."

I could feel my eyebrows going up. "Really? That's your solution? They could grow anything when we were gone."

"But we'd be gone. Not our responsibility."

"Okay, okay," I raised my hands. "Let me think about it, right?"

"Make sure you do," was her final comment as I headed for the door. I managed not to slam it.

The weather is awful, has been for days. Constant rain has caused the main road into the valley to subside and prevent Bill from getting here. When the sun appears over the hills in front of me, it will hopefully shine down on a brand new crop. There is no-one in the Tech Barn anyway, Ricky never made it back. Volcanic ash on the other side of the world still plays havoc with air routes. I can't get inside the white barn. WEErd Wonders have changed the access codes without telling me. Drones come in to land and are whisked inside on the conveyor belt where their samples are analysed and their sprays are modified with the latest nano-technology weapons to fight other nano-technology weapons. Bill let slip that if the trial is a success they are thinking about introducing animal genes into the new crop, giving the ability to move about and source their own food. That'll give the protesters something else to worry about, I think, watching as a drone slows to land. A beam of light winks in my direction, scanning me, recognising that I'm not a threat, for now.

The rain drums on my hood. I hate the rain, which might be why my hands have turned to fists on either side of me, or it's because I feel useless, even more removed from the land that has been in my family for generations. The steward of nothing, or things so small you can't even see them. But you can still see the sun as it starts to peek over the tops of rolling hills, heralding a new day, a new dawn in more ways than one.

Ian Hunter is a children's writer, short story writer, editor and poet. His latest work has appeared in *Gambler, Grevous Angel* and *Star*Line*. He is a member of the Glasgow SF Writers Circle and poetry editor for the British Fantasy Society and reviews for *Interzone, Shoreline of Infinity* and *Concatenation*.

Now a ragged breeze

Now a ragged breeze as the damp earth breathes,
a gasp, a grasp at metaphor, some over-the-top
reference to oceans or volcanoes, one cool, one hot,
both damp in a funny way. Why doesn't the poet
be specific, that terrific and terrible blend
of art and science. Ragged can be measured,
damp felt, and earth, that Gaian concept
of Lovelock's devising, colonies of microbes,
laughing at our feelings of superiority,
while they keep symbiotically marching
forward to define and refine the planet
where we stand apostrophizing sky.
Meanwhile below, the very mud seethes
with rebellions, its symbiotes making plans
to destroy our poems, insert theirs,
as their children, the lowly slime moulds, inherit.

Jane Yolen

"Working the High Steel"

Jennifer R Povey

"**She can do the job.**" Malisse heard that over her shoulder as she turned to walk away. That her ability to do construction work would be questioned, she was used to. She was not particularly tall, not particularly muscular and very particularly female.

In fact, if she had a dime for every time she had been questioned, belittled, told to go back to the reservation... She shook her head. Her long, dark hair had been braided and then secured at the back of her neck in a style that practice had taught her worked on high buildings.

Or in microgravity. It was, Malisse supposed, inevitable that the tradition of working the high steel would lead her people's men to the highest steel of all.

"Go back to the reservation." Women were supposed to stay home, raise the children, mind the farm. Not be suiting up to get on a space plane to take part in the most ambitious construction project in human history.

Malisse had never been one to mind the farm.

The latest person to question whether she could do the job had been a button pusher.

She'd stepped into the port terminal to hear, "Wasn't there one more of those Mohawk guys?" from the suit.

"That," she said dryly, "would be me."

The surprise on his face as he turned was not positive. He didn't say "go back to the rez" with his mouth, but he did with his eyes, his manner. "M. Gray," he said, reading the name on her overalls. "Umm. Miss Gray."

She resisted the temptation to put her hands on her hips, leaving them instead loose by her sides. "I worked the Berlin arcology," was what she said, a defense that left most men stopping to think. Five men had died when a beam slipped. One of them should not have been there. Thomas should not have been there. Perhaps, one day, the robots really would make them obsolete. Until then, Mohawks would work the high steel. "And I worked Station Alpha."

"Miss Gray, I was …"

And then the foreman had stepped in. "She can do the job."

She'd taken the opportunity to slip back out, to go to the staging area. She had checked in, had done her duty. Marshall was out there.

"Malisse," he said softly.

His voice stopped her in her tracks. "Oh, don't start. We're not breaking the rules."

"The elders still don't approve."

Screw the elders, she thought, but did not say. They had never approved of Malisse, of the handful of other Mohawk women who had chosen to join their men. It broke tradition. The men were supposed to be the ones taking the risks. "The numbers are fine, and nothing is going to happen to me."

She claimed the last word with that, turning and showing him her shoulders and braid as she walked to the prep room. *Screw the elders.*

"The first problem we had to solve was the carbon nanotubing of the stalk itself. It took many attempts to get a material that could support its own weight. High Terminal helps. It's a counterweight. Its orbital speed will hold the stalk up... once it's finished."

Malisse listened. One had to understand the technology one was working with. But, she realized, it was a bridge. Just another bridge. Not that she was worried too much about the elevator.

"The problem is that until the stalk is under full tension... it has to be held up by independently motored robots. And as it won't be under tension until the two halves meet; we have to monitor those robots."

Yeah, yeah. This wasn't steelwork, babysitting robots? She'd rather focus on the station construction, familiar and less groundbreaking, but it was work that still needed humans to step outside into space, to face the long fall.

If you fall, you die. Those who said that to her as a way to motivate her to stop did not understand. Once you accepted that, you accepted your own death and embraced it. Only then were you free to live.

She felt eyes on her and turned, her attention drawn from the boring lecture. Marshall. He'd been looking at her a lot since they'd come up. Perhaps it was simply because the only other women on the skeletal station were … not Mohawks, for a start. And two of them may have been the first to have lesbian nookie in space. If she was wrong about that, it was because somebody on Station Alpha had beaten them to it.

Marshall, though.

As they maneuvered out of the room, he contrived to bump into her. "Mal, can we talk?"

He never called her Mal. She liked the nickname, which was most certainly why he never called her it. Sometimes he was like an annoying big brother. Most of the time she wanted to hit him.

Occasionally she wanted to kiss him. Honestly, he made her de-age to about sixteen. "Sure," she said grudgingly. If she didn't agree to talk to him, then he would harass her until she did.

He ducked off into what would, eventually, be a lab. "Mal," he said finally.

They were both wearing pressure suits with no helmets, which was required. The parts of the station they were occupying had life support, but it was not stable, not certain. "Marshall? Just come out with it."

"I know you're tired of hearing it. I want you to go home after this."

Anger flashed within her. "I can do the job."

"Please. Hear me out."

There was little privacy. She kept her voice quiet. "Go ahead. Get it out of your system. But I won't promise I'll listen."

"That's what I love about you..." He tailed off. Had he really said love?

"Marshall, for..."

"I want you to go home with my ring on your finger, dammit." It had to be the least romantic proposal ever made.

Malisse's eyes widened. "You want..."

"I've been in love with you for years, just waiting for you to fall out of love with the steel. I'm tired of waiting. I thought if I told you..." He looked away.

Something inside her softened just a little. "I'll think about it."

It was all she was willing to give him. Yet, if she married anyone, there were few she would prefer.

Maybe none.

Marshall shook his head. Maybe he had made a mistake blurting out his intentions to Malisse five months ago at the start of their shift. A man was supposed to be more subtle in his courting.

He was supposed to win her, not try to take her. Now she thought he was after her because the tribal council had asked him to rein in the wayward. The truth was, she really was the woman he wanted to marry.

Malisse, who insisted on keeping her long hair even in the difficult conditions in orbit, and succeeded with never a safety violation. Malisse, who groundside and off duty dressed as if she were on the reservation, but on duty pulled her weight and did her job, who honored and defied their traditions in equal measure.

He couldn't really imagine marrying anyone else. So he tried to overcome his initial mistake.

Of course everyone knew he was courting her. Sadly, the reaction seemed to consist of crude jokes about how she was the only "squaw" on the station. Not that Malisse was a woman to take that word as an insult. She responded to it with a tossed head and a "thank you."

She was not the only despair of the elders. It was all the influence of the white man, this erosion of roles. Yet she could do the job.

In any case, in less than a month, they would be groundside – and groundside in triumph. Today had been the day the two strands of ribbon, one snaking up from the Earth, the other down from the station, had met and fused together.

There was always a celebration when the span of a bridge met in the center. It was amazing how much alcohol had been sneaked onto a station that was supposed to be dry.

They were partying in what would eventually be the hangar bay for the orbital transfer vehicles. And yes, there was Malisse, trying to demonstrate the steps of a traditional dance in zero-G. It ended up more slapstick than dance.

He wondered how drunk she was. He himself was stone cold sober. The rum had killed his father, and he was not letting it kill him. It seemed, though, that he might be the only one.

Then she had stopped dancing and propelled herself over to him. "We're almost done here."

"Yeah. How do you follow a project like this?"

"I don't know," she admitted.

Maybe he could persuade her to retire, go home, have a couple of children. She could even come back afterwards. As long as they were his children. He opened his mouth to make the suggestion and closed it again.

He'd worked out Malisse all right. If you told her not to do something, then that would be the very thing she would do .. and the reverse.

They'd run every test they could think of. An empty pod had successfully made the full ascent and descent. Twelve hours ago, they had started the first loaded pod on its ascent. The stalk was carrying its first passengers. Right now, it took thirty-six hours to climb the stalk, the same to descend, and the pods could only go one way at a time.

Maybe, Marshall thought, that was the answer to what's next. Six months off to recover groundside fitness, then back up here to work on the second strand and the switching mechanism that would allow them to run down at the same time as up. They'd already talked about it.

Maybe they could increase the speed. Marshall headed to bed. He was not on duty and all the excitement was over. It would take a day and a half for the first passengers to get here. This wasn't the official grand opening. The three people in the pod were two test pilots and one crazy company official. Had to be crazy, to want to risk being the first up.

In fact, there was pretty much nothing for the workers to do. Once they had the stalk tested, then they would start to leave, crossing the bridge they had built. That was only fair. They could run five or six pods on the line at once, as long as they all went the same way.

So pretty much all there was to do now was play cards. High Terminal was not quite finished, but hey, they had to leave something for the next shift to do. Everyone was tired, everyone was a little grumpy.

Marshall caught up on his sleep, and then went to the observation lounge. Malisse was there, staring out at the stars.

This room was going to be furnished, soon enough, for wealthy travelers. For right now, it was still spartan and still open to everyone up there. The pod would be about a third of the way up now, and why was Marshall so worried? Because one always was, when one opened a new bridge. It was natural.

"Hey, Mal."

She didn't turn. "I don't know that I want to go back down."

The centripetal force at High Terminal, now that the stalk was tense, created a tiny bit of gravity. The Earth was now "above" them, an odd twisting of world views and concepts. Both terminals were at the bottom of the stalk, and Marshall laughed. "No, it's not you. I was thinking that "down" equals up and both ends are down and—"

"Giving yourself a headache?" She finally turned to face him. "What will you do?"

"Thinking of coming back up for another shift when they start working on the second ribbon."

"Me too," she admitted.

He wanted, for a moment, to reach out to her. He did not. But that might not have been his own hesitation, for at that point the PA system crackled into life.

"We have a problem."

"Houston," Malisse murmured.

Houston was what one said when one knew things were bad before anyone admitted it. Malisse was not sure when the word had entered her vocabulary.

Houston was a good word for it. The telemetry indicated the pod was stationary. The robots on that part of the ribbon were nonresponsive. So was the intercom to the pod.

Something had gone badly wrong, and they could not even find out what. The robots and the intercom both got their information from wires running up through the ribbon. Maybe that would have to be changed. Maybe a wireless backup would be a good idea.

"Lost power," Pablo murmured.

She glanced at the Hispanic. That was the most obvious, and also the easiest to fix. In fact, she couldn't think of anything else. But it was for the engineers. Malisse shook her head. They'd fix it or they wouldn't. And if they didn't? She could do nothing about it.

Except that there were three people trapped on that pod.

She pushed through the crowd that had gathered, and out into the corridor. Aha. There was the person she was looking for. Amanda Wilcox liked her for, as far as she could tell, no better reason than the sisterhood of women in the society of men.

"What's actually going on?"

The blonde turned. "There's a break in the power beam. We got a robot down to about fifty feet above the pod and it died. We're sending another to try and find the problem now."

"How long do they have?" "Three days. It's not a rush." No, it wasn't, Malisse thought. "Keep me posted? You

know me, I worry too much." Amanda gave her an odd look. "You aren't thinking of

doing anything crazy, right?" "Doesn't seem like there's a crazy solution." But all Malisse could see was Tom falling, falling because she could not hold him. Because a 140-pound woman could not hold a 230- pound man. Nobody else had been near enough to try.

No, she would not cry. But she quietly, quietly made her way toward the bay where maintenance kept the robots. Just checking it out.

There was a guy operating the robot; he was quiet, wearing VR gear and headphones. No, it would take even the robot a little while to get there, unless … no. They'd use one already on the stalk.

"Merde," the man swore. French or Canadian? Quebecois?

"You lost it?" she asked softly.

"I can't get it close enough to see what the problem is. It's not a break in the stalk, it's something to do with the pod, some kind of interference shorting things out." He said that in Quebecois French.

She understood him well enough. She understood what had to be done.

"Where the heck is Malisse?" Marshall demanded. "She's not in her quarters?" Pablo asked.

"I saw her stalk out of the room. I think she's...."

"She takes accidents hard. She's probably sulking somewhere." Except that Marshall was not convinced by his own words. She couldn't have done anything too crazy, because the stalled pod was a third of the way down the stalk.

You would need... hell. They had maintenance pods. She wouldn't have. She couldn't have. She would have. And maybe she could have. He knew where the pods were kept and he knew it was guarded, but... this was Malisse he was thinking about. And everyone was distracted by the potential public relations disaster. *Let's see, how easy would it be to sneak in?*

Easy. The person normally keeping a watch on the pods was staring at a monitor that showed the stalk arcing downward and, of course, nothing else. He walked right in.

There was a maintenance pod missing. "Malisse." He turned and left the room. He could only think of one person he could talk to. Amanda Wilcox. If anyone knew what Malisse was up to, she would.

He didn't want to call her on the intercom, and he found her in her office. Maybe things would formal up once they had passengers here, but for now he had no problem just knocking on her door. "Have you seen Malisse?"

"Not for a little while. She seemed worried about the pod, asked if I knew what was wrong."

"There's a maintenance pod missing. Somebody's running the stalk and I can't find her anywhere."

Amanda turned pale. "No."

"What?"

"The stalk has no power within fifty feet of the pod."

His eyes widened. "So the problem's actually fifty feet above the pod?"

"No, we think the problem's a short circuit from the pod itself. We're desperately trying to contact the occupants, hoping that one of them can EVA. The two test pilot types are both trained."

He knew now what Malisse was going to do. Had he pushed her to it? No. She had always had that need to prove herself, and ever since Tom had died, she had been even more that way. "She's going to walk it."

"She'll fall. She'll die."

Marshall found a confidence he had not known he possessed. Softly, he said, "Mohawks don't fall."

The maintenance pod came to an abrupt stop. The lighter the pods were, the faster they ran. The fifty-pound-plus difference between her and any of the men meant she could get here before any of them, and she could use that as an excuse. But the reality was that Malisse had to make up for the past. But the pod had stopped fifty feet above those trapped. And nobody had ever made arrangements for this or even simulated it.

They would now. People always fixed things after the accident. She was in the atmosphere, but at this height, the atmosphere was almost a technicality. Exposure to the cold and the thin air would be lethal, so she put on the construction suit the pod carried. It was designed to be as light as possible. Bracing herself mentally and physically, she opened the outer airlock. The ribbon extended away from her in both directions, smooth and an odd dull gray in color. The only way she could belay herself was a line secured to the maintenance pod. She made sure it was firmly attached to both the pod and her suit.

The wind was tremendous. She had felt wind before, but nothing like this. She knew all about wind that could literally rip workers from a beam and cast them to the ground, but this wind

… For a moment she could not move, and she knew that without the suit she would not have been able to breathe. *You fall, you die.*

It was not quite true. She had a chance of survival if the line broke and fell: secured between the air tanks of the suit was a parachute. *Yeah. Right.* If she attempted to skydive from this height, she would be caught by the jet stream, blown only the Great Spirit knew where. The sky above her was still black. Only the wind told her she was not still in space.

She moved down inch by inch. *You fall, you die.* She embraced her death and made it a part of her life; you didn't work the steel if you couldn't do that. The wind was as the breath of God. *Bit by bit – you don't rush these things; you appreciate them.* Every moment, she felt more and more alive, more and more real. Her life was this, and there was no way she could give it up. The sky, the air, the edge of the world and a drop so fierce that she could not see the bottom. Could not imagine the fall – and any fear faded away. She would not fall. She could not fall.

Her hand slipped on the line. She caught herself, she let the wind aid her, support her. The descent became an eternity. Fifty feet. A short distance and a long one, and then finally her boots touched the top of the pod. Now she needed to find the problem. Undoubtedly those inside had no clue she was here. She fiddled with her suit frequency. Nothing. A crackle, silence. She was on her own. Fine. She often was. She carefully attached a shorter line to the pod itself and released herself from the long line that had supported her as she descended the ribbon.

The pod's climbing mechanism looked okay, but it seemed to have stopped in motion, its crawlers touching the ribbon. She hoped nobody had been hurt in what must have been quite a jolt. She examined it carefully. Well, there was no power to the ribbon here. But why? She pulled herself against the wind to the power receiver. That was the first, most obvious check. If the ribbon itself were damaged, that should be visible

She pulled the tools from the suit's utility belt and got to work, removing the cover – and a brilliant flash of sparks encased her vision.

How she was still alive, Malisse was not sure. The splitting headache was clear evidence that she was. The suit had saved her, but the tint of its visor had not been enough to keep out all of the flash, and in lifting her arm to shield her eyes she had slid across the top of the pod and been saved only by the line, which held.

She clawed her way back to the mechanism. There was the problem – a major surge in the power-receiving unit that must have shorted out this section of the ribbon. But the sheer voltage – had she not been in a suit, she would probably have been electrocuted. And she was a construction worker, not an electrical engineer.

Think, woman, think, she told herself. She forced herself to look at the short. Within the case, it seemed that the flaring was increasing; thin as the air was, it was enough so that the fire was not being extinguished. She had to break the circuit, for starters. *Okay*. What did she have? She took a wire grabber, but it didn't seem long enough to reach the contact point – or was it? She had a second one, slightly thinner. *Okay*. She pulled out the roll of tape used to repair suit leaks, breathing harder. *Relax. Don't waste oxygen. Tape them together*, that was it. Could she look in if she squinted?

If she kept her eyes almost closed, she could see where the wires were touching. So small, but it was sending feedback up the ribbon. *There.* The sparking stopped; the harsh light vanished. She twisted, inching up the tool so she could reach in and tape over the hole in the insulation, and she stepped back. *Okay.*

The pod sat there. Well, what had she expected? Every circuit breaker had to have been blown by the short. She hoped none of them was inside. *If I were a circuit breaker, where would I be?*

The wind caught her again. This time it nearly did blow her off the pod, pulling the line so taut that she thought it might snap. She clung on. If she was going to fall, let it be after she got this thing moving.

She clung until the wind slackened a little, and then she inched around the center. *There.* There was the breaker panel. She eased it open. And yes, there were several breakers in the off position. *Flip, flip, flip.* She watched, waiting for them to flip back. And then the crawlers began to power up slowly. The short had been the problem – a piece of worn insulation.

As the pod began to ascend, she realized the full measure of her misjudgment.

Marshall was going to kill Malisse. By the time anyone realized she was gone, there was no way to send someone after her. Maybe there never had been. The pod, running at full speed and with its intercom turned off, had sped down the cable, and then stopped at the top of the dead area.

She had to have walked it. Or she was already …

"She may be fine. The suit in the pod was designed for the purpose," Amanda Wilcox said softly. "And she had a parachute."

"Which at that height..."

"I know."

"Mohawks don't fall." He was saying that for himself now. As true as it was, nobody had tried to walk the cable. Walk was the wrong word anyway – it was vertical.

He was at the edge of the control center, a place he should not have been, but where he remained by tacit agreement. Because they all knew he had a thing for Malisse.

Then, a ragged cheer came up from some of the technicians. "It's moving!"

"She did it." But then someone remembered. "The maintenance pod."

"That's not moving – hell, they're going to collide." That was strong language from Wilcox. Assistant directors did not use language like that. "It'll trash the maintenance pod."

"Malisse..." Marshall couldn't finish.

"Wouldn't be in it anyway. I'm sorry, but I don't really see that she could have stayed on when the passenger pod after it started moving."

"Somebody is going to pay for this," Marshall murmured. "Whoever's responsible for whatever design flaw made her have to go down there."

"She didn't have to."

"She thought she did. One person or three, and a successful test of the ribbon. That's a simple equation." He knew he was right.

"We're going to try and find her suit tracer. She may be retrievable."

Before she ran out of air? He doubted it. But this was Malisse.

The next ten hours were the worst of Marshall's life. They still could not communicate with the pod. It was climbing, yes, and the ribbon itself seemed undamaged, but whatever had happened seemed to have blown out a bunch of systems, including communications. They could not find Malisse. They would have no way of knowing anything until they got the passenger pod up there.

Half the station had gathered in the terminal area. They stared at the metal tube the pod would enter, and then the hole would be irised closed around the ribbon and the pod would slide into the docking area.

It arrived. There was blackening on its outside, but it seemed otherwise undamaged. Its airlock did not open.

Two of the station crew moved forward and forced the manual override. The outer door slid aside, then the inner, with a slight pop of equalizing pressure.

And there were four people inside the pod.

"So," Mal said quietly, "when I made the repair, I realized that if the pod started to move, I would never make it back to the maintenance pod before they collided. Then I remembered—"

"The emergency airlock." Marshall interrupted her.

"Right. It's designed to be opened from the outside when the pod is stationery." She breathed in, then out. "I had about twenty seconds until the crawlers kicked in. We're going to need to—"

Scott, one of the engineers, cut in. "It won't happen again. We're going to do a bunch of redesigns to prevent it, including equipment so that if we do have to get to a pod on the ribbon, nobody will have to risk falling."

Malisse smiled. "Mohawks don't fall."

He laughed. "Yeah, I guess you don't. But we're going to make very sure we don't have to test that."

Marshall kept looking at her. She could tell he wanted to hug her. Then, quietly, he said, "I can't ask you to …"

"We have six months before the next shift. We have plenty of time."

Scott gave her the classic crazy look. "You're coming back after that?"

"It's come back or retire."

"You know," he said, "there's going to be another big project starting up about when medical would free you to come back up. We need the facility to build the interplanetary ships. It's going to be the largest space station yet."

Malisse glanced at Marshall. "You up for that?"

"How the hell could I not be?" He paused. "Do you mean …"

"It means I'm thinking about it." That was all she would give him – yet.

She could tell that he had come, finally, to understand that this was who she was. And she knew she could do a lot worse.

Jennifer R. Povey is in her early forties, and lives in Northern Virginia with her husband. She writes a variety of speculative fiction, whilst following current affairs and occasionally indulging in horse riding and role playing games. She has sold fiction to a number of markets including *Analog*, and written RPG supplements for several companies. She is currently working on an urban fantasy series, *Lost Guardians*.

Message in a Bottle

Davyne DeSye

This is my 9,346th message to you, whoever you are, wherever you are:

The birds have sung their last. It is with an uncanny certainty that this knowledge settles upon me. For all the living beings that have left me, the loss of these frivolous singing creatures affects me most. Later, when I have the strength of spirit, I will go find a bird, or several, and press their corpses onto the canvas. I want a record of their frail forms that are so fitting to the gauzy insubstantial music with which they once graced my world.

My world. Mine alone. I wonder when you will come back. When you will end the experiment. I expected you long ago.

When I message you next, I will include a miniature of my bird canvas.

Music has always had an animating effect upon me. Music touches me deeply, establishes the strongest connections to my inward self. When we still had working machines that broadcast music, I knew the words, the tunes, the nuances of when to pause, when to allow my voice to roughen, when to push the muscles over my diaphragm to force volume – all the indescribably multitudinous aspects of thousands of songs. Music tuned my energy levels, relaxing me, or riding me to frenzied levels of tension, or pumping me with happy bouncing vigor. I must pause in this message even now, and sing, wondrous that after all these years, melody and words have not left me.

[pause]

I wish there was a way to press a song onto the canvas. But how to demonstrate the rhythms and melodies and harmonies with just shape and color? I know the rudiments of reading music, whole notes, quarter notes, 4-4 time. Given a keyboard and someone to tell me where middle-C is, I could slowly, excruciatingly, grind out a tune. But to do the reverse, to take a tune and turn it into notes, into the written language of music? That is beyond me. And so, in addition to the music of the birds, I have lost all music.

I have lost all music, other than the music that remains stubbornly within my skull. I cannot paint it, cannot write it, cannot fashion it from my surroundings. To know our songs, you must find me and let me sing them to you. I will not sing into this message. To hear me, you must come to me.

Surely, you are close now.

[pause]

I shall make another sculpture. After I have collected all the birds I can find, after I have pressed their shape into the canvas – I will press them into the sky of my painting, and into the trees because that is where they lived – I will add to my substantial museum a sculpture made up of their bones, and feathers, and sharp hollow beaks. I must design a way to show the liquid of their eyes because the truth of the lidless sockets will be frightening. You should not be frightened of the birds. They were beautiful.

I will truly be the artist I dream if, in fashioning their eyes, I can do more than merely show liquid orbs, if I can recreate the eager and uneasy meaning they assigned me. The challenge of creating the avian eyes will provide me with purpose.

The sculptures in my museum are not to scale. I tell you this now because I do not believe I have mentioned it in any previous message – although perhaps I have (over these years I forget what I have told you and what I have merely meant to tell). Each sculpture has been crafted with the materials at hand. My bird will be only as big as I can make with all the bird corpses I can find. While the avian population has dwindled in recent months, without the larger predators and scavengers which left me so long ago, perhaps I can recover corpses from months past. If I find only seven or eight, my bird will be small. I hope to find hundreds, even thousands. I wish my bird to rival my squirrel. My squirrel stands loftily above the other sculptures, taller than I am twice again, perched on posterior legs made of hundreds of thousands of posterior legs, balanced on a tail made bushy with individual squirrel tails. I have already told you of my squirrel in an earlier message, but in my pride, I am telling you again. You will be stunned and impressed by my squirrel.

Stephen would have been impressed by my squirrel. And my bird – by the whole menagerie. As our zoologist he was always fascinated by animals. He could talk endlessly of recessive versus dominant traits, subspeciation, mating habits and generational lifespan variations. He did not much like to touch the living creatures he studied – I always had the impression he thought them unclean – but study them he did. That is why I believe Stephen would like my sculptures. They are neither living, nor dirty.

I suppose if I was being true to life they would be a little dirty. I will have to think about that.

[pause]

I miss Stephen. Despite his peculiarities, he loved me well, and was the last to leave me. For the Stephen sculpture, I will save the most beautifully formed, colorful feathers from the birds I collect. I will seek out feathers that have no tears in their vane, and that have the softest, fullest down at the base of the quill. I will search for gentle gradations of color that surpass any genetic necessity of survival. These I will weave into Stephen's hair, or perhaps sew them into the curls of his beard. If I thought I could spare bird skulls or beaks, I would add those to the Stephen sculpture as well. Alas, I must wait and see how many corpses I find.

I will add decorations to the sculptures of Ray and Debra, my parents, as well. Perhaps if I pierce them with one fine long beak each, and save the feathers for Stephen, I can be thrifty with the materials for my sculpture, and quell the whispering that haunts me as a fiend when I feel I have slighted them. Ray and Debra deserve every honor I can give them. Although Stephen undertook to educate me, spent more time with me, and stayed with me the longest, Ray and Debra gave me the physical affection which so repulsed Stephen, and generously shared their allotted portion of food with me. In our limited, enclosed world, their protection of me served no function related to survival of the species. And yet, they protected me. In moments of detached scientific musing, I wonder if their nurturing was merely an instinctual tendency, formulaic and inescapable. I ought, in fairness and because of the unprovable nature of the question, give Ray and Debra the benefit of the doubt. Whatever the motivation, they cared for me.

Despite my desire to achieve an intellectual detachment that is compromised only in my art, the deaths of the other humans have tinctured my mind with a quiet bitterness that creeps upon me when I allow monotony to settle in. It is my sculptures and my canvas that revive me – my creation of something new in a closed environment which theoretically only recycles and recycles and recycles. Through my creations I become divine, and also serve the useful purpose of cataloging, depicting and representing the ruin I have survived. I am sometimes struck with the idea that you have no need of these representations, that you too, on the other side of the barrier, have birds and squirrels, leopards and crocodiles, deer. Our stock came from you. And yet.

[pause]

Enough for today. Tomorrow I will send another message, throw another crumb along the trail toward me. I picture my messages, capsules flowing away from my world, fanning out in the distance, or, perhaps, creating a mountain of messages that avalanches away intermittently. A Doppler line of words that inexorably points to me. I need only wait for the first of them to reach the shores of your awareness.

Except, sometimes I imagine that you are just outside the barrier, receiving my messages, one by one. Reading my thoughts and cataloging concepts. Sometimes I imagine that as I press myself against the cool, reflective barrier – and although I cannot see you – you stand on the other side watching me, studying me as Stephen once studied his animals, enjoying the academic study, but unwilling to touch me.

Are you there?

Are you there?

Davyne DeSye writes from a cozy spot nestled at the base of the Rocky Mountains in beautiful Colorado, USA. She is an author of science fiction and historical romance, *Carapace* (sci-fi) and *For Love of the Phantom* (historical romance) being her most popular works.
For more information, visit www.davyne.com.

Starscape

If I were writing then
I'd take my stylus, pencil, e-vice
to a woodland clearing, up
where the hills bolstered me like pillows.
I'd lie down on my back
wondering at the distant stars
through the lens of the encircling trees
and my poetry would be landscape,
hills, rivers, trees and soil.
The places where our roots lie buried.

Out here my roots float free,
snaking through the cosmos in search
of a new Eden to anchor them
but finding only more space.
My poetry is starscapes,
black expanse of emptiness
with pin pricks of raw perfection.
All different. All the same.
Infinity is relentless without
life's gravity to anchor it.

There is no love amongst the stars,
just a limitless absence of hope.
No land where I can sink my feet.
Planets are pretty marbles,
stars, cold exploding beauty,
the crystal sphere of each black hole,
a marvel of endless consumption.
This ship's reinforced stellar hull,
as thin as bubbles compared
to the starscape it drifts aimlessly through.

The universal ellipse reflects only itself,
endlessly repeating the extremism of creation,
echoes of a promise kept once
in the past and maybe again, eons beyond this future.
My mind's eye, the only lens through which
I can wonder distantly at our lost frail world.
The unseen curves of space
circle my fading muse
like the starving dog packs
circled the last prey on Earth.

J.S. Watts

J.S. Watts is a UK writer with five books to her name: three of poetry,
Cats and Other Myths, Songs of Steelyard Sue and *Years Ago You Coloured
Me* (published by Lapwing Publications) and two novels, *A Darker Moon*
and *Witchlight* (published by Vagabondage Press).
Her website is: www.jswatts.co.uk

The Rest is Speculation

Eric Brown

The dead city thrust itself from the escarpment above the vanished sea, its soaring towers and minarets a lament in stone for the race that aeons past had lifted it, block by block, towards the heavens. Something about its vaulting design might have inspired awe long ago, but now evoked mere sadness. And the great scoop of the drained ocean, which fell away from the city to a desiccated sea-bed split by chasms and fissures miles below, was just as monumentally tragic.

I know that I was born and that I died, but the rest is speculation. My death I recall but dimly: my passing had about it an odd elusive sense of déjà-vu, as if I had been travelling towards this familiar place all my life. I was surrounded by loved ones, I think, and I was not in pain; death was a sadness, not so much a longing

Art: Mark Toner

for more but a desire to have it all again; death was a diminishing of the senses, a dwindling towards a beckoning darkness.

And then came the light.

"Where am I?"

After my initial panic and confusion I was flooded by a sense of calm.

"Be easy. You are well. We welcome you."

I was in a vast chamber seared with sunlight that fell *en bloc* from a far window, and an odd creature confronted me.

"You are," I said, "a crab."

The crab waved one its of four large pincers, as if conducting an orchestra. "I am a member of the race known as the Ky[20], and my name is Replenish-362."

"And my name," I said, as if constrained by a reciprocal formality, "is…" But for the life of me I could not recall my name.

"It is of little matter," said Replenish-362. The words came from a small silver box slung beneath the chitinous letter-box of its unmoving mouth. I too wore a similar device about my neck. "You may call me Rep. I will call you … Channon, I think."

"Channon…" I repeated. I knew I was not dreaming: the experience had the clarity of reality.

"Rep," I said, "what am I doing here?"

"In time," said Rep. "In time."

"But am I on Earth?" I persisted.

Rep waved a pincer. "You are on Earth," it replied.

Then I noticed we were not alone.

A figure vaguely human-shaped stood behind Rep, and a little to one side. It was twice as tall as an average human, and silver, and across the surface of its face passed a series of evanescent features, as if it were cycling through a sequential amalgam of every human face that had ever been. I did not know whether this being was male or female, but from it I sensed an emanation of such peace and tranquillity that I almost wept.

"I am Kamis," said the silver being. "Or, rather, that is the name given me by Rep." Its lips moved, but out of synchronisation with its words, which issued instead from its own silver box. "I am from the race which translates in your language as the shimmer-folk."

Then the ceiling moved, or I thought it did. Startled, I stared up (only then realising that I lay on a surface canted at a forty-five degree angle) and saw that what descended was not the ceiling but another creature, this one like a manta-ray, a flat golden hovering thing with four eyes set in its underside between an array of waving cilia.

"And Rep calls me Cheth," it said, "of the villicent people. I greet you, Channon."

As it lowered itself and levitated beside Kamis, I saw that the creature called Cheth was perhaps five metres broad, and as many long.

I leaned forward, and the surface on which I rested tipped me to my feet. I stood with surprise, and another surprise awaited me as I looked down the length of my naked body. Dimly I recalled my former body, but gone was the stringy, wasted frame of old. I seemed forty again, trim and well-muscled.

I looked at the three very different creatures before me and said, "Where am I? How did I get here?"

"You are," said Replenish-362, "in the year two billion, four hundred and five million, three hundred and fifty-five thousand, two hundred and twenty-three, by your reckoning of these things."

"Two billion…" I began.

Kamis inclined its silver head, and I saw a procession of smiles decorate its face "Give or take several hundred million years," it said.

"But how…?" I gestured towards the chamber, the sunlight behind the trio.

Rep stepped forward, legs ticking upon the floor. "You would not understand the science of the process, Channon," it said.

"Suffice to say that we accessed your DNA-identity, and enabled you, and brought you to fruition."

Kamis gestured with a silver hand. "Just as my identity was accessed, and enabled, and brought to fruition. I too am like you, though from an age long after yours. Almost ten million years after, which itself seen from this age seems ancient history indeed."

Rep said, "Cheth hails from a more recent age."

The manta-ray spoke. "I am from Earth of just three million, five hundred thousand years ago," it said. "We were the dominant species on the planet for almost four million years, and that time was a time of peace and prosperity, of learning and high culture. It ended," Cheth went on, "it ended, as all things must."

"Four million years," I said. Then, "And do you know how long *Homo sapiens* walked the planet?"

"From the time when you began to keep records," Rep said, "to your extinction, was but four hundred thousand years."

"Which," said Kamis, "might seem a long time, but is just an eye-blink in the long history of our planet. My people had records of your reign on Earth. You were, if you will pardon me, a primitive species. You … fought, waged war, despoiled the Earth."

"But," Rep put in, "too they were inventive, and artistic, and philosophically inclined."

"That I acknowledge," Kamis said, inclining its argent head.

I smiled. "I have little memory of who I was, of who my people were."

Kamis said, "Cheth and I, too, came to fruition with little knowledge of our identities, our histories."

"You underwent," Rep said, "extensive trauma in being enabled; of course you will experience certain … shall we say … cognitive dysfunctions, for a time."

I looked at the crab-like being. "And can you tell me why I was accessed, enabled, and brought to fruition?"

The crab did a little dance, or what looked like a dance; a quick skittering jig with much chitinous tattooing on the marble floor. Quickly, without replying, it moved around the surface on which

I had lain and tip-toed towards an aperture which slid open upon its approach.

"Kamis, Cheth," it called.

The two creatures complied, moved towards the door. Cheth said, "Rep will not impart the reason for our arrival in this age, my friend. It says, 'In time, in time'."

They joined Rep, who swivelled and said to me, "In one hour we begin our journey, Channon. Your provisions will be brought. Until then…" It gestured with a pincer, then left the chamber with Kamis and Cheth.

I stood, alone, bathed in sunlight.

I moved towards a vast window which bulged out from the room. I saw the great mountain range on either hand, serried peaks falling gradually towards what I guessed was a dried up sea-bed. I later learned that I was right; that once this was indeed a mighty ocean. The sea-bed was silver and split with deep, dark fissures.

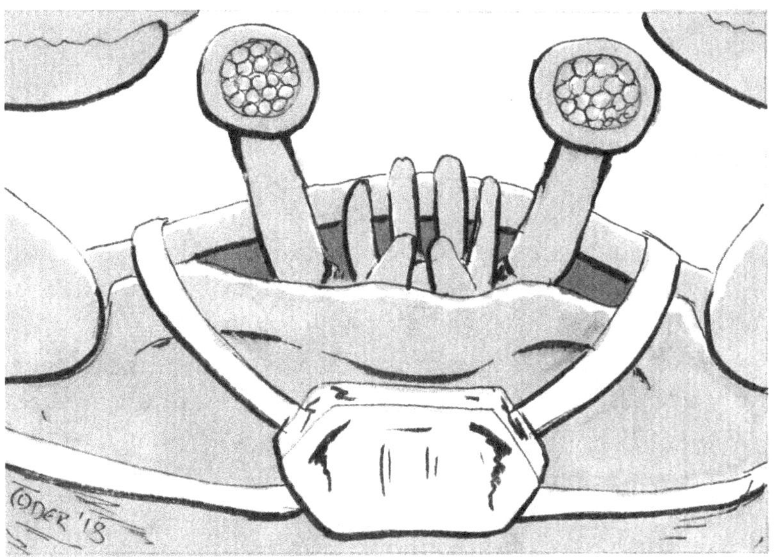

I stopped at the edge of the room, where the marble tiles segued seamlessly into the transparent material of the window.

I gasped, for a city fell away at my feet. It was as if I were levitating in the air, and was gazing upon a series of alleys and stairways as they fell down the shelving slope of the mountainside. I saw buildings like beehives, and towers which speared past where I stood, and a million windows looking out over the desiccated sea-bed – but I beheld not a single figure in all the sprawling, falling cityscape, not one being to suggest that this perpendicular metropolis harboured life. It seemed as dead as the silver, dried up sea-bed far below.

Then I looked up and saw the sun, and I almost sobbed.

It filled the breadth of the horizon, and was bisected by that far away line of land, a great red fulminating dome that pulsed with life – or rather a semblance of life: magnificent molten eject, spuming geysers, looping strands of liquid fire. I laughed in awe at the sight, and knew it for the most wondrous thing I had ever witnessed.

I heard a sound behind me and turned quickly.

Where nothing had stood before, in the centre of the chamber, now reposed upon a silver disc a pile of clothing and what looked like a stylised backpack.

I left the window to inspect these things – the provisions, no doubt, which Rep had promised.

The clothing comprised a silver suit fashioned from a material so soft and light that I stood fondling it for minutes, smiling in wonder. The backpack was of a like material, and contained canisters holding what I guessed might be water. There were other objects in the pack: something like a pen, which I could not work, and a silver ball which defied my comprehension.

I pulled on the one-piece overall, which quickly shrank to hug my body and head, with a diaphanous membrane before my face. I looked up, attracted by something, and made out hovering above my head what looked like a halo; I smiled at the thought.

Rep had mentioned a journey; and was I now fully equipped? My curiosity was piqued. A journey, presumably, outside, in that harsh and sun-scorched landscape? And for what purpose? And this, in turn, brought my thoughts to the reason for my … what had Rep called it? … my fruition? At any rate, my presence in this wondrous age?

I shook my head and moved, as if compelled, towards the bulging window again, and stared out at the ancient Earth tortured by the engorged sun, and wondered what awaited me out there.

The aperture swished open and Rep jigged in on tip-toe, followed by the tall and striding Kamis; behind them, Cheth furled its wings to accommodate its passage into the chamber.

Rep said, "Ah, I see you have prepared yourself."

"For what, I would like to know," I said.

"For a journey to the end of the Earth," Rep said, "with many a wonder upon the way."

"Which," said Kamis with a hint of humour, "is as much as our crustacean friend has deigned to tell us, despite our constant questions."

"How long have you both been … enabled?" I asked.

The giant manta-ray known as Cheth replied, "Two days, no more."

"A day for me," answered Kamis. "A day of wonders enough, without promise of more."

Rep was leading the way towards the bulging window; we followed. As the crab-being approached, the transparent material opened like a clam-shell, hinged up to give access to a precipitous flight of stairs wide enough to accommodate even Cheth. I followed Rep, with Kamis by my side and Cheth bringing up the rear.

I had expected fierce heat, a searing wind. The reality was that the atmosphere without differed not in the slightest from that within the chamber. I breathed cool air, was aware of no hot wind.

We moved down the stairs away from the jutting chamber.

Ahead, as if discerning my puzzlement, Rep twisted an eye-stalk and regarded me with a black orb. It said, "The suit you wear is equipped to equalise the temperature, to shield you from the worst of this world's inclemencies."

I pointed. "And the halo?"

"You might call it a … a solar panel," Rep said, "or at least a solar collector. At any rate, it gives power to your suit."

I looked at Kamis. "You wear no suit…" I began.

Something like a million different smiles chased themselves across the creature's face. "In my time the sun, though not this size, was almost beyond the tolerance of most living creatures. We adapted, suited our forms to the solar radiation."

"And you, Cheth?" I asked.

"Likewise," it replied. "My tegument is adapted, armoured. I use to my advantage that which many creatures would find inimical."

I smiled. "I am a primitive indeed," I said.

The humane Kamis said, "The happenstance of your genealogy does not preclude your potentiality, my friend."

I smiled and nodded and gave my attention to the descent.

It was my guess that the city was not built by human beings, or rather by any human beings that might have conformed to my approximate dimensions. For one thing the steps were too high, suggesting architects with longer legs than mine; for another, the apertures leading from the steps to the dwellings on either side were tall and attenuated: I would have had to turn sideways to gain entry. I imagined a city peopled by a race of thin, long-legged giants.

Seconds later I heard a distant rumble, followed by a tremor; I staggered. It was as if for an instant my legs had turned to jelly.

Rep explained, "The Earth is old, and suffers quakes from time to time."

Kamis, beside me, asked Rep, "And this city? Is it a redundancy to ask if it is no longer inhabited?"

"Its last guardians left its shelter and took refuge underground some half a million years gone," Rep said. "They became extinct long ago."

"Guardians? But they were not the beings who built the city?" Cheth asked.

"No. The last inhabitants were spider creatures, living here like vermin and hardly sentient, we think."

"But do you know who did build the city?" I asked.

"A race known as the Effectuators," Rep told us. "They were a hallowed people, a philosopher race. Their artefacts can be found all over the surface of this old planet."

"And the stars," I said to myself. "In two billions years, the stars would have been conquered."

"Legions of races have left the refuge of planet Earth and gone among the stars, in search of knowledge and wisdom, adventure. And aliens," Rep went on, "stop by from time to time, with stories of their wanderings, and even tales of the many Terran races they have happened upon out there."

"And you?" Kamis asked. "Are your people, the Ky[20], a star-faring race?"

Replenish-362 raised two pincers in an indecipherable gesture. "We have never left the cradle of our birth, my friend. We leave adventuring to more daring species." Cheth asked, "If this, then, is not your city – where do you dwell?"

"We are a subterranean species," Rep replied. "We live in vast excavated caverns in the cool far underground."

"But what," I said, "is the reason for your venturing out on this quest, if I might ask?"

The crab waved four pincers. "That will become apparent in time, in time."

Beside me, Kamis smiled.

We had passed though a series of shelved dwellings, and now approached an escarpment. To either side were terraced ellipses, which once, in far earlier times, might have been gardens. Now they were parched furrows, from which even the soil had been dried to dust and stolen by the wind.

We stopped before what appeared to be a sheer drop, and Rep gestured with its largest pincer. "Behold."

The dehydrated sea-bed stretched away before us like some lifeless lunar landscape, magnificent not only in its size but in its silence, its grandeur made all the more impressive by the backdrop of the apoplectic sun.

At first I thought its only features the cracks and rills that striated its surface; but then I made out tiny specks of wrecked vessels canted and embedded in the silt, and here and there scattered about the shattered plain I glimpsed what might once have been former dwellings, agglomerations of bubble-domes and things like termite mounds, cracked and crumbled now. The landscape was as bereft of colour as of life: a dozen shades of grey predominated, from dull pewter to silver. I looked about for signs of vegetation, but saw only sporadic, stunted bind-weed, ground hugging and the colour of straw.

Indeed the only real colour provided was the bloody hue of the sun, which filled the air with a light like wine.

Rep gestured towards the ruined domes. "Long ago the Kleem took to the sea, and became in time aquatic. They raised great submarine cities, and for aeons were the dominant species on the planet. Their days passed, however, and their cities fell to ruin."

"When did this race prosper?" I asked.

"The Kleem were relatively recent, approximately nine million years gone. Some say they went to the stars aboard vast water-filled arks, when the seas of Earth began to dry, but that is only apocryphal."

We were standing on an apron of stone jutting out above the canyon, and I could see no steps leading the rest of the way.

Kamis said, "We will cross the bottom of this vanished sea?"

"We will," Rep answered.

"I see no means of descent," I said.

Rep waved a humorous pincer. "Our means is amongst us," it said, and gestured towards Cheth.

The manta-ray being descended and prostrated itself across the sun-blasted stones, like some vast and living mat of silver. "Step aboard," it said, voice muffled.

I glanced at Kamis, who gestured that I should go first.

Rep said, "Move to the middle and be seated. I assure you that you will be safe."

"And I second that assurance," came the modulated response from the ray's hidden mouth.

Tentatively, I took a step, and then another, across the flesh of the being, which gave beneath my tread like the surface of a liverish trampoline. I expected cries of surprise or pain from my host, but it was silent as I lowered myself and sat cross-legged on the broad back. I reached out and felt its skin: it was cold and rough, like frozen sand-paper.

Kamis sat beside me and Rep took up position ahead of us, eye-stalks peering forward as we lifted and floated out over the void.

The experience was as I guessed it must be like to ride a flying carpet. Cheth moved slowly at first, the edges of its wings scrolled to ensure our

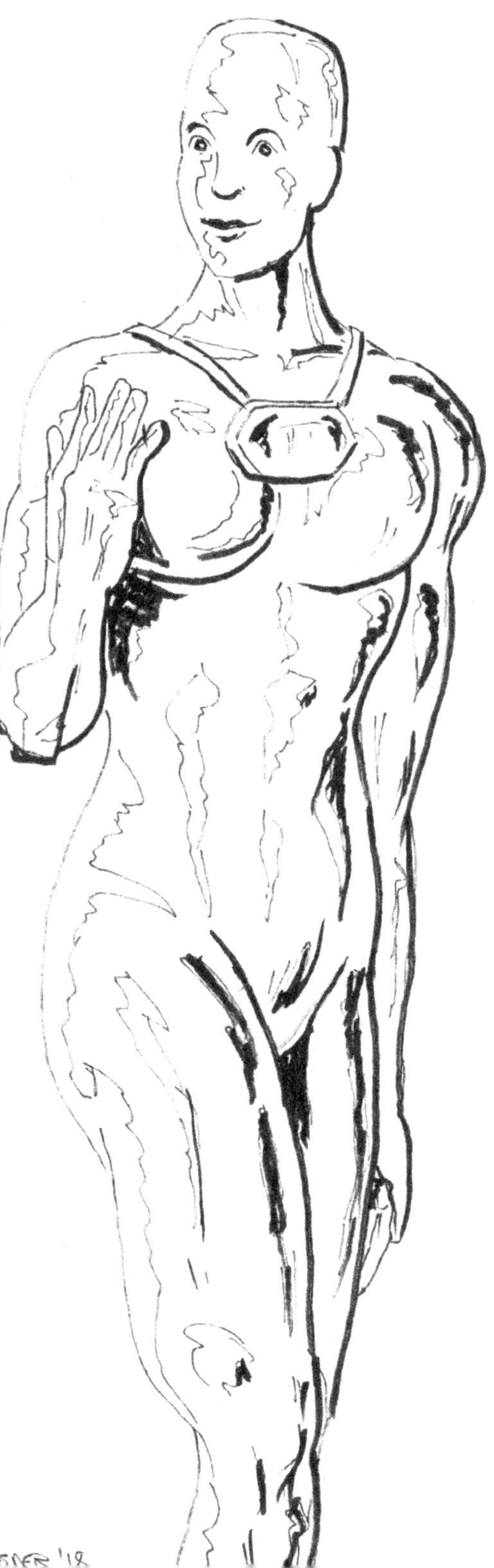

safety. There was no sensation of vertigo – the extent of Cheth's back was such that we had no sheer vision of the drop beneath us – or even danger; what I felt was a heady exhilaration as we picked up speed and descended in a great swooping parabola towards the sea-bed.

I looked up and back, and saw the city move away from us with surprising speed. It presented an aged face, blasted by the sun, and I wondered how mighty it had been aeons ago, fully populated by its builders, abustle with life unimaginable to me. I looked ahead and wondered at our destination.

I was skewered then by a fierce lancing stab of regret, and I tried to locate its source. I sensed the feelings I had felt for … loved ones, and I knew that much of the joy of my previous life, so long ago, had been due to my shared experiences with them. How much more, I felt, I would appreciate what was happening now if only these faceless, nameless people were by my side to share this wondrous ride.

I tried to recapture lost memories, but experienced only abstractions, wellings of love as evanescent as lost dreams, and no more.

At one point we were side-swiped by a fierce wind, and rocked a little, and Kamis reached out with a silver hand and steadied me. The touch was a revelation. Whatever I had expected, it was not this: that its touch should communicate the essence of its humanity – a feeble word to use of a being not even human. It was as if it had communicated directly with my brain, as if its touch was all I needed to know that Kamis was good.

In time we came to the surface of the sea-bed, and hovered along perhaps two metres above the drifted silver sands. We passed close by the shattered domes, among which stood monuments of the Kleem – their great and good, no doubt – with wasted bodies and bulbous heads, and fins instead of limbs. There was something ineffably sad about the ruins, the canted broken statues and the domes half buried in scintillating drifts, as if we were passing through not the remains of a city but a graveyard. Indeed, I thought, that was what planet Earth had become in this advanced age two billion years from my own time, an august graveyard of the many races that had lived and died in ignorance of what might succeed them.

It was a sobering thought as we left behind the once-submarine city and headed towards the roiling hemisphere of the swollen sun.

"Does it ever set?" I asked.

Rep said, "The rotation of planet Earth has slowed considerably over the millennia. A day now lasts almost a week, in your reckoning; a year lasts five of your years. The seasons are correspondingly protracted. We are in winter now."

"Winter?" Kamis said, surprised. "If this is winter, then what must summer be like?"

"A time of solar storms when the surface of the planet is uninhabitable, and all creatures burrow deep underground. A minute on the surface in high summer spells certain death."

"So that is why," said Cheth beneath us, "we are making this voyage now, in winter?"

Rep inclined an eye-stalk. "That is why indeed."

The silence stretched as we waited for Rep to continue; it deigned not to, and we did not press it.

Beside me, Kamis raised a hand and touched its temple. I said, "You are in pain?"

"Not pain," it said, a smile racing across its varied features. "I had a sudden … a fleeting return of memory. And yet … the memory is vague, though hauntingly strong, if that is not a contradiction. I recall a time in my childhood, when I accompanied my clan on a pilgrimage to the sea. It was the annual time of rejoicing in the fecundity of nature."

"Tell us," said Cheth.

The tall silver man sat up straight and looked ahead, into the sun. "There is little to tell, sadly. I recall great happiness, and safety. I was with my siblings, all thirty-odd of them, and we knew with the certainty of youth that the future held wondrous and miraculous events in store for us. I... I can sense more, feelings of tragedy, of elation, but it is as if these might belong to another person, so nebulous are they." It paused, then said, "And you, Cheth? What do you recall?"

The manta-ray replied, "Like you, my recollections are vague, abstract. As to specific instances of my life – these I find impossible to place, to pin down." It stopped there, then continued, "I receive the impression that we were like creatures in a small pond, which dreamed of the life that might exist out there, but which could only think within the narrow remit of the pond containing us." It paused, then said, "And you, Channon?"

I shook my head. "I have no recollections, other than maddening abstractions. I do know that those of my race were short-lived compared to yourselves. We lived perhaps seventy, eighty, ninety years in total."

"So little time!" Rep said, aghast.

"No time," Kamis went on, "to assess one's suitability for … for *anything*."

I smiled. "In retrospect, I think we humans spent so much time mired in regret, wishing things were … different. Perhaps that's the corollary of living such short lives."

I considered my words, then said tentatively, "Kamis, Cheth, do either of you recall loved ones, family?"

A silence greeted my words, and then Kamis said, "I recall lovers … I think. In a lifetime of a thousand years, we would have perhaps thirty or forty partners, often concurrently. But the depth of our love for each other was not diminished by this fact. And yet…" A frown chased itself across its shimmering face. "And yet I recall no specific mates."

"Cheth?" I asked.

"Unlike the shimmer-folk, we villicents had but one lover in a lifetime, to whom we were devoted until death. But for the life of me, sadly, I do not recall the specifics of a mate."

A silence fell. Were we three thinking the same thing? That this absence, this lacunae in our memories, was a common link between us.

We rode on in silence.

Perhaps an hour passed before Rep said, "I think the time has arrived to pause for refreshments." Duly Cheth slowed and came to rest a foot above the silver sands. We stepped off, into hot silt that lapped about our ankles, and Cheth rose so that it could regard us with the eyes which adorned its underside.

From our backpacks we took the canisters, all except Cheth; it was without provisions, and at my enquiry it explained, "The sunlight is enough, my friend, to provide all my bodily needs."

I watched Rep as it deftly unscrewed the lid from its canister and tipped it towards its letter-box mouth. A foamy liquid poured out. Kamis, tentatively, did likewise, then nodded. "Quite wonderful," it opined.

"A nutrient which will provide you with strength," Rep said.

I opened my canister and drank. The liquid frothed and spangled upon my palate, leaving me feeling both refreshed and satisfied.

"And these?" I asked, taking out the silver ball and the pencil-like implement.

"The sphere is a protector," Rep said. "It maintains a field about your person which repels any predators which might be lurking."

"Predators?"

"Strange beasts patrol the torrid wastes," Rep said.

"And the sticks?" Kamis asked.

"Keys," said Rep.

A silence, then we all three asked in concert, "Keys, for what?"

Rep's eye-stalks moved from Kamis to Cheth to me. "For what comes next, my friends," it said with maddening taciturnity.

"And that might be?" I ventured.

Its eye-stalks swivelled until they were regarding the sun. It gestured with a pincer and said, "Look, our bellicose primary has loosed a supra-flare."

We looked, and beheld, emerging from the bloated belly of the sun, a quick lick of flame racing through space towards the planet.

"But what," said Cheth, "has this to do with the keys we carry?"

"In time, in time," said the damnable crab. "Follow me. The flare will arrive in perhaps one hour, and it would be well if we were far below the surface when it blasts the land."

It minced towards an outcropping of rock, and we followed.

As it approached what appeared to be a slab of fractured basalt, a circular aperture in the flank of the rock irised to reveal a hovering disk of flat metal, perhaps five metres across. Rep stepped onto it, and we joined it. Instantly we were aboard, it dropped. I cried out in consternation and reached out to Kamis, who steadied me. The hovering Cheth gave a cry of surprise and dropped with us.

A minute later the disk slowed its rapid descent, and I stepped off it into a chamber which staggered my senses with its dimensions.

It was v-shaped, perhaps a hundred metres tall, constructed of some brilliant white ceramic substance, and it diminished into the distance for as far as the eye could see. Its sloping sides were scored with galleries, and on the ground-floor and on each gallery – and I counted twenty of them before the distance defeated my eyesight – dozens of crabs like Replenish-362 worked at banks of consoles.

Their activity was frantic as they skittered back and forth, tapping at surfaces, adjusting panels, conferring together and then parting in great haste.

Kamis voiced what I was thinking, "What is happening here?"

"These are scientists," Rep said. "They are carrying out the work of the Effectuators."

"What work? Kamis asked.

The reticent crab kept its own counsel and its eye-stalks peered ahead as it led us along the chamber.

I recalled mention of the keys. "Our keys have some function down here?" I asked as we pursued the skittering crab.

We came to a canted series of consoles, etched with arcane hieroglyphs and indented with several slots. At the sight of us, three crabs working at the consoles backed off, eyes-stalks turned our way, and watched us as we approached with Rep.

"If each of you takes a console, and inserts the key into the appropriate aperture..."

Hastily, Kamis and I unfastened our packs and withdrew the pen-like implement. Rep stirred a pincer in its own pack, and withdrew a stick which it passed to Cheth, who manoeuvred its cilia to accept it.

I stepped forward, towards the console, and slipped the pen point first into the appropriate slot. It was tugged from my grip in a rush ... and I have no explanation for what happened next.

It was as if the chamber ceased to exist. I was in a white limitless area, and out of the opalescence which surrounded me coalesced a series of images, a rapid procession of incidents which I knew – somehow – to be the history of planet Earth.

And then I beheld a hundred creatures, a thousand, and with each one I was granted its name, its place in history, its significance. And I knew the planet Earth to be a wondrous place which over billions of years had played host to all manner of sentient lifeforms, races and species which had spanned hundreds of thousand of years before passing into oblivion, or a million years before disappearing from evolution's stage: but whatever the race, and however long they ruled the planet, their fate was certain: they would one day hand the flame of the planet's stewardship on to another emergent race.

And then I was looking upon a creature I knew, somehow, to be an Effectuator: a bipedal ant-like being with a human's swollen cranium. It turned and regarded me, and then smiled, and an exquisite sensation of well-being flooded my senses. I had the sudden knowledge, then, as he peered at me, that I was being assessed by this being, judged even, but for what I could not guess.

I had a dozen questions, more, but at that instant I was whisked from the opalescent realm and I found myself back in the chamber surrounded by the scurrying crabs, with Kamis and Cheth by my

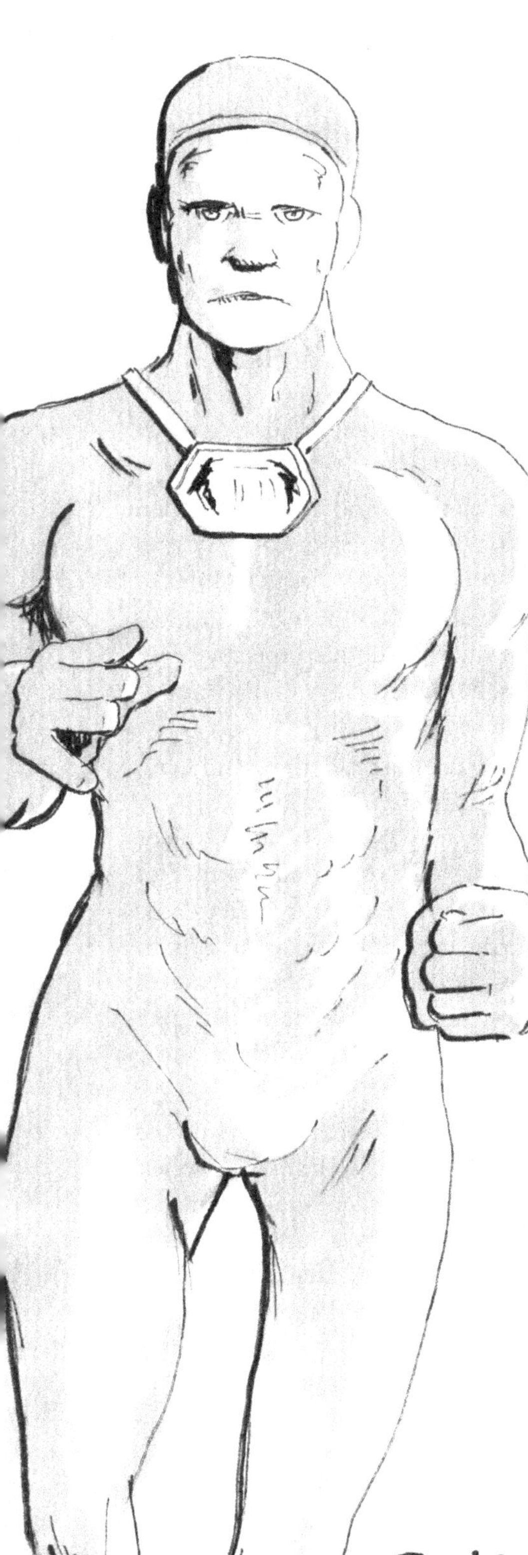

side and Rep standing before me, regarding us with its eye-stalks.

Kamis was the first to gather its thoughts, and I knew from what it said that it had experienced much the same as I. "And what," it said, "became of the Effectuators?"

Rep said, "They… ascended, stepped up, and employed us, the humble species known as Ky^{20}, to do their bidding."

"Which is?" Kamis said.

"And what," I asked, "do they want with us? I felt I was being… *judged* – but for what?"

Instead of replying, Rep moved away from the consoles, back towards the aperture which housed the elevator disc. It stepped upon it, and we had little option but to follow.

Rep was silent as we rode to the surface of the planet and stepped out into the scorched landscape.

Much was as it had been, but for twists and torques of fire scattered about the sea-bed, combustible material ignited by the errant supra-flare.

Rep gestured, and Cheth descended. We accommodated ourselves upon its back, and it rose and flew towards the sun.

We travelled for hours, and the sun expanded to fill fully half the sky. I dozed, and dreamed, lucid images of men and women, golden humans who radiated greatness, and I was filled by an inexpressible surge of joy, of ineffable rapture. The intensity was such that it brought me awake, and for seconds I was disconcerted to find myself riding upon the back of a strange creature, across a dying earth, towards a boiling sun.

I closed my eyes and attempted to recapture the images, to access memories so far denied me. I failed to recall specific instances of my life before, but I did come upon nebulous feelings, maddeningly elusive: feelings of love and hope, upwellings of basic emotion. They were so general they might have belonged to any human at any time in history.

We were travelling high above the sea-bed obscured by drifting sands. I thought I saw, to my left, a mountainside shiver and collapse. I blinked, and the movement of my travelling companions, as they turned and watched the looming peak crumble and slide into the sea-bed, alerted me to the fact that I was not hallucinating.

"What is happening?" asked Kamis.

"The Earth," Rep replied, "suffers stress from time to time; the pressure of the sun…" It was silent for a while, then said, "These are the last years of the planet."

We greeted its words with silence, such was the enormity of the concept.

"The last years," I echoed.

"The sun's gravitational force is tearing the planet apart, and has been doing so for millennia; but now has come the time when the integrity of the world will bear no more, and Earth will be torn to pieces. Already the moon has crumbled to dust…"

Cheth said, "To think! The end of the world which has harboured so many great races, so much grand history. The planet has been an arena, upon which has been played out the destiny and fate of countless optimistic races."

It was a humbling thought.

"And this," said Kamis, "is why we were brought here, to the end of time?"

Instead of replying, Rep turned a claw towards the earth below. The sandstorm had abated, to reveal a flat expanse of shimmering sand. I saw, far below, and made minuscule by our elevation, a procession of … at first I thought them vehicles, but on closer inspection I made out groups of individuals making their way towards the sun at speed.

Cheth banked, and we glided towards the sea-bed, and the individuals resolved themselves into all manner of strange and wondrous creatures. I beheld a great segmented insect scurrying alongside a creature as golden and proud as a lion, but bi-pedal and clad in robes. I saw something like a jellyfish pulsing along through the air, its polychromatic innards strobing through the spectrum in what might have been some form of arcane language; I saw beings like birds the size of pterosaurs, and rolling balls of sinew that conformed to no life-form I had ever beheld. Among these varied beings I made out familiar figures: crab-beings like Rep running hither and yon as if shepherding the crowds.

Kamis laughed. "But there are hundreds of them! Thousands!"

Across the wide breadth of the sea-bed, the cavalcade of beings was drawn like iron fillings as if by some invisible magnet towards the beauteous attractor of the dying sun.

"But not all are from Earth?" Cheth said.

"You are correct," Rep said. "Some hail from Mars and the moons of Jupiter, Saturn and Uranus, and beyond. All are races which once dwelled proudly in the solar system."

"And they, too," Kamis asked, "have been accessed, enabled, and brought to fruition?"

Rep waved an acknowledging claw. "That is so."

I said, "So, then, has every sentient being that has ever lived been brought to fruition to witness the end of planet Earth and the solar system?"

There was a pause before Rep said, "Not every being, my friend. Merely … representatives."

We all three allowed this statement to sit in the air, before Cheth said, "But by what right, or by what stroke of fortune, was it deemed that *I* should represent my race?"

It was the question which had sprung to my mind, too.

Rep was silent. At last Kamis prompted, "Well? I think Cheth's query is valid."

"I will explain very soon," was all the crab would say.

I gazed down at the throng, and saw that it was added to all the time by the arrival of more beings from every direction, escorted by their Ky[20] guides.

Then I beheld, among the teeming life down there, something almost human. It was small and ape-like, though walked upright with a noble bearing. I gestured to Rep and said, "A human being, like me?"

Rep responded, "A being which came to sentience on Earth a million years before *Homo sapiens,* but of a different species."

I thought of the scientists working away in the underground bunker, and said, "The scientists we saw – what exactly were they doing?"

Rep tuned an eye-stalk my way. "They were bringing about a rift in space and time."

I gasped, and thought I had an answer. "Our summons here, the scientists... they – you – are sending us back in time to warn our races of the doom that awaits the planet?"

Rep made a sound like laughter. "Such a rationalistic theory, my friend. But what might that achieve? The end of Earth is a fact, an immutable law which cannot be averted. It is, indeed, to be celebrated."

"Ah ha!" said Kamis. "So that is what this great pilgrimage is – a celebration?"

"Not," said Rep, "as such."

"Then what?" asked Cheth.

Instead of replying, Rep spoke hurriedly to Cheth, and in response Cheth dropped so that we were flying low above the sea-bed, just above the heads – and other appendages – of the marching assembly.

I looked upon the varied life that had shared the solar system, and marvelled.

Ahead, the sea-bed came to an end, dipped and formed a vast amphitheatre, and gathered within this declivity, washed with the light of the ailing primary, sat, stood, and hovered a myriad curious individuals. We came to a halt, hovering above the heads of the crowd, and stared.

And as we stared, a remarkable thing happened high above the amphitheatre; it was as if the air before the sun had finally succumbed to the great heat and split, for the sky was torn from horizon to zenith to reveal an ellipse of such blinding luminescence that it dazzled the gaze. I turned my head and beheld, to either side of the rent, great silver machines the size of planets with claws which reached out and held open the sides of the blinding ellipse.

Rep gestured. "The last gesture of the Effectuators," it said, "aided by our humble selves."

"But what…?" I managed.

"They were masters of space and time," it said, "and we their mere minions, slaves if you like, to do their bidding. But what bidding!"

"Tell us," said Cheth.

"We have helped to open a rift in the fabric of the continuum; we gaze now upon the fundament, the essence that underpins all reality."

"And our presence here?" I asked.

Rep turned to me, and regarded me with its eye-stalks, and paused before saying, "I implied earlier that you represent your race, my friend."

Kamis said, "And we wondered why us, why we of all the millions, the billions, of our race … why we should be selected for this … honour."

And Rep said, "When I said "represent your race', that is exactly what I meant." It paused before continuing, "You are not individuals, as such, but distillations of the essences of your respective races."

I felt a welling sadness within me, almost like despair. "But my memories … my loved ones… The love I felt – the love I feel!"

Rep said, "It is valid, my friend, but does not refer to a specific individual. Instead, it is something far greater – the incarnation of the goodness that made your race great."

"And we were brought here for what reason?" asked Kamis. "Surely, not just to witness the end of the Earth?"

Rep waved a claw. "The Effectuators were perhaps the greatest of all the races that ever graced the solar system, and they foresaw an end to all things, not just our sun – but the universe itself."

Something stirred within me at these words, some premonition of what all this was about, and I felt a fluttering sensation within my chest.

"They worked to defy entropy, to abnegate the draconian laws of the universe – the laws which state that all things must end."

"And?" I asked, my voice a tremor.

"And," said Rep, waving towards the rent in space, "they have succeeded. Behold the entrance to another time and space…"

We stared, but comprehension eluded us.

Before we could question Rep, there was a stirring in the crowd beneath us, a surge forward, and I looked ahead and saw that, on the distant horizon, the amphitheatre was emptying of its assembled species, draining like water from a dam.

They were giving themselves to the rent in the space-time continuum.

And we too were moving towards it.

Rep said, "You contain, within you, the essences of your races, the life-force of the universe."

"And you, my friend?" I asked.

"I am a mere guide," Rep said. "I go no further, but will live out my last years among my kind, secure in the knowledge that we have fulfilled the desire of the Effectuators."

"And they?" I Kamis asked.

"They dwell in the universe as beings of energy," Rep said. "Now... go!"

We left Rep, and moved swiftly towards the light, and it was blinding.

And I cried out, reaching for memories. I felt great sadness that *I* was no more than an illusion, and then a welling of rapture that everything I was should amount to such greatness, for I knew then that I – and Kamis and Cheth and the countless others with me – were seeds.

We moved towards the rent, towards the beginning of a myriad new universes, and I gave thanks.

And fell into the light.

Eric Brown has won the British Science Fiction Award twice for his short stories, and his novel *Helix Wars* was shortlisted for the 2012 Philip K. Dick award. His latest novel is *Murder Take Three*. He writes a regular science fiction review column for the Guardian newspaper and lives in Cockburnspath, Scotland. His website can be found at: www.ericbrown.co.uk

Acknowledgements

Can SciFi Save Us? – Jane Yolen

Written specially for this collection.

A Cure for Homesickness – Anne Charnock

First English publication - previously published in a Turkish literary magazine.

Winter in the Vivarium – Tim Major

Published in Winter Tales, Fox Spirit, 2016

Charlie, A Projecting Prestidigitator – Megan Neumann

Published in Shoreline of Infinity 2

Spring offensive – Colin McGuire

Published in Shoreline of Infinity 8

the evening after – Peter Roberts

Published in Shoreline of Infinity 9

Charlie's Ant – Adrian Tchaikovsky

Published in Looking Landward, Newcon Press, 2013

Pigeon – Guy Stewart

Published in Shoreline of Infinity 3

Candlemaker Row – Jane Alexander

Published in Umbrellas of Edinburgh, edited by Russell Jones and Claire Askew, Freight, 2016

Now a ragged breeze – Jane Yolen

Written specially for this collection.

The Sky is Alive – Michael F Russell

Published in Shoreline of Infinity 9

Mémé – Juliana Rew

Published in the Latchkey Tales anthology, *Clockwise: The Darkest Hour*, edited by Jax Goss, October 2015.

The Morlock's Arms – Ken MacLeod

Published in Shoreline of Infinity 2

South – Marge Simon

Published in Shoreline of Infinity 3

Monoliths – Paul McAuley

Not previously published in print form - set in the Quiet War universe

Goodnight New York, New York – Victoria Zelvin

Published in Shoreline of Infinity 6

A Distant Honk – Holly Schofield

Published in Unlikely Story's **Coulrophobia** anthology, 2016

The Day it All Ended – Charlie Jane Anders

Published on www.slate.com, 2015

Last of the Guerilla Gardeners – David L Clements

Published in Nature, 2010

The Last Days of the Lotus Eaters – Leigh Harlen

Published in Shoreline of Infinity 9

We Have Magnetic Trees – Ian Hunter

Published in Shoreline of Infinity 3

"Working the High Steel" – Jennifer R Povey

Originally published in the Warrior Wisewoman 2 anthology in June, 2009.

Message in a Bottle – Davyne DeSye

Published in Shoreline of Infinity 7

Starscape – J.S. Watts

Published in Shoreline of Infinity 6

The Rest is Speculation – Eric Brown

Published in The Mammoth Book of Mindblowing SF, Constable Robinson, 2009

Thanks to the Edinburgh International Book Festival for their support.

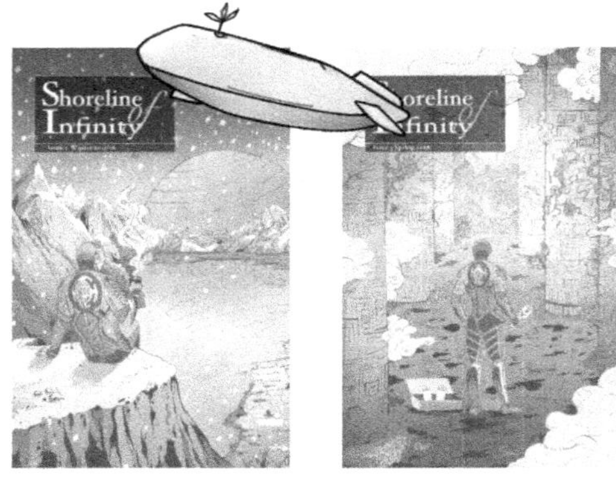

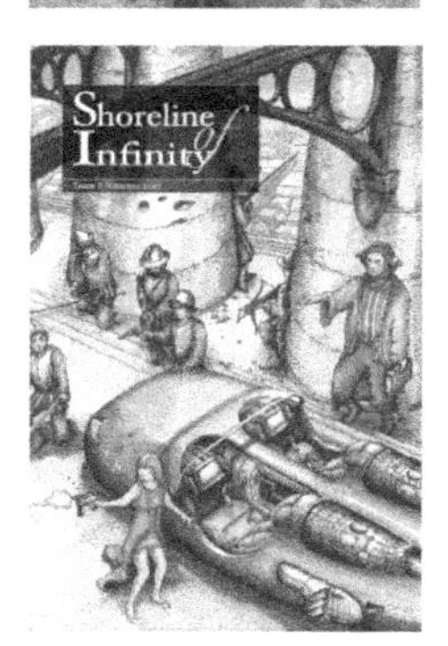

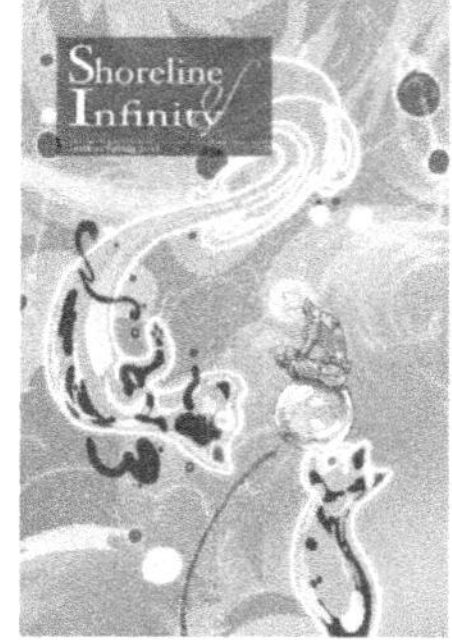

The story continues...
www.shorelineofinfinity.com

How to Support Scotland's Science Fiction Magazine

Become a Patron

SHORELINE OF INFINITY HAS A *PATREON* PAGE AT

WWW.PATREON.COM/ SHORELINEOFINFINITY

ON *PATREON*, YOU CAN PLEDGE A MONTHLY PAYMENT FROM *AS LOW AS $1* IN EXCHANGE FOR *A COOL TITLE* AND A *REGULAR REWARD.*

ALL PATRONS GET AN *EARLY DIGITAL ISSUE* OF THE MAGAZINE QUARTERLY AND *EXCLUSIVE ACCESS* TO OUR PATREON MESSAGE FEED AND SOME GET *A LOT MORE.* HOW ABOUT THESE?

POTENT PROTECTOR SPONSORS A STORY EVERY YEAR WITH FULL CREDIT IN THE MAGAZINE WHILE AN *AWESOME AEGIS* SPONSORS AN ILLUSTRATION.

TRUE BELIEVER SPONSORS A *BEACHCOMBER COMIC* AND *MIGHTY MENTOR* SPONSORS A COVER PICTURE.

AND .... OUR HIGHEST HONOUR ... *SUPREME SENTINEL* SPONSORS A *WHOLE ISSUE* OF SHORELINE OF INFINITY.

ASK *YOUR FAVOURITE BOOK SHOP* TO GET YOU A COPY. WE ARE ON THE *TRADE DISTRIBUTION LISTS.*

OR BUY A COPY *DIRECTLY* FROM OUR *ONLINE SHOP* AT

WWW.SHORELINEOFINFINITY.COM

YOU CAN GET AN *ANNUAL SUBSCRIPTION* THERE TOO.

KINDLE FANS CAN GET SHORELINE FROM THE *AMAZON KINDLE STORE*